BLUE VALENTINES

By Laura Moe

Blue Valentines
©2019Laura L. Moe

Contact information: www.lauramoebooks.com
Twitter@Lauramoewriter

Book clubs: for discussion questions visit www.lauramoebooks.com
This a work of fiction. Any resemblance to actual persons, living or dead, is purely coincidental. While some locales actually exist, most are fictional.

Cover design by Ashley Nicole Conway

Summary-*On the verge of graduating high school, Michael has two choices: remain in Rooster, Ohio, and attend a local college, or accept a scholarship to a workshop in Seattle with a chance to meet his long-lost father. In either scenario, Michael risks losing his relationship with girlfriend Shelly.*

Subjects:
Contemporary YA—Fiction | Love—Fiction | Relationships—Fiction | High School—Fiction
Parents—Fiction | Families—Fiction | Friendships—Fiction | Young Adult—Fiction | Heartbreak—Fiction | Seattle—Fiction | Writing Workshops—Fiction | Dysfunctional Families—Fiction | Breakups—Fiction
DDC-FIC

ISBN 9781073346783

Praise for BLUE VALENTINES

Love mends broken hearts, but can it heal damaged souls? Fans of contemporary romance will root for Michael and Shelly as they navigate high school graduation and a summer that changes everything.

Louise Cypress, author of BITE ME

In BLUE VALENTINES, Laura Moe delivers both a terrific sequel to her celebrated debut, Breakfast with Neruda, and an equally strong stand-alone story. This poignant exploration of love and loss sparks with sharp humor and enduring lessons on the healing nature of writing.

Steven Parlato, Author of *THE NAMESAKE* and *THE PRECIOUS DREADFUL*

This follow up to BREAKFAST WITH NERUDA is everything I hoped for. Laura Moe really delivers! –
Penelope Wright, author of NO USE FOR A NAME *and The Collapse* Series

Chapter One

April 1
Michael

Shelly reaches for the poster advertising Pelee Peugeot's latest novel and upcoming appearance, and I clutch her wrist before she can mangle it.

She gives me a sheepish grin. "Just this once?"

"Nope." I lead her inside the bookstore. "My little Miss Demeanor."

"You're one to talk."

Last summer, Shelly and I met when we served community service together. Footage of my arrest is on YouTube if you want to see it. I got expelled for bringing fireworks to school to blow up my ex-best friend's car. You might say I have anger issues.

Shelly figured out pretty quickly I also lived in my car. A normal girl would run like a man on fire from a guy like me. But hardly anybody accuses Shelly of being normal. Besides, I'm a magnificent kisser.

Funny how we didn't have a thunderbolt moment when we met. We didn't even like each other. More like Shelly and I grew into one another like ivy on a brick wall, and now I can't imagine life without her.

"Pick out any book you want," she tells me inside the store.

"I still don't know why we're here. It's not my birthday, *or* my *un*birthday."

"It's National Poetry Month, Neruda," she says, using the nickname she gave me. It's also my surname on my fake ID. Shelly wraps her hands around my bicep, a move designed to soften whatever blow she plans to hurl at me. "It's my way of celebrating."

"Yeah, right. You're probably planning some fractured April Fool's joke."

She scrunches her face. "I'm not!"

Our first real date was here at The Book Loft in Columbus. Every time we come here, I ask for a map because the bookstore has thirty-two rooms.

She glances over my shoulder at my map. "Let's start up in Poetry and work our way down."

We weave our way up the narrow staircase. On the poetry shelves I scan a few titles, but none of them pulls at me. My brain is elsewhere. School is over in less than two months and I have no idea what to do with the rest of my life.

Shelly yanks my sleeve. "Let's go visit Fiction." We meander over to rooms eight, nine, and ten.

"Why did I know you'd head straight for your boyfriend, Jack Kerouac?" I ask.

She sticks her tongue out at me and moves down a couple of shelves. She grabs a copy of *Norwegian Wood* by Haruki Murakami. "Ooh! Here's the book we need for our lit class." She and I are finishing high school at the community college. The good thing is, it's a thousand times better than the melodrama of Rooster High. The bad thing? Shelly and I hardly see each other all day. The only class we share is Contemporary Lit.

I shrug. "Okay."

Shelly scrutinizes me. "What's up with you today? Normally you're like a crack addict around books."

I lift a copy of the Murakami book from the rack. "I don't know. Trying to figure out the rest of my wretched life."

"Today is your lucky day because I have a plan for you."

I roll my eyes. "Can't wait to hear this."

Shelly snags me and hustles me toward the staircase. "C'mon. Let's go have coffee."

We wind our way down to the checkout and Shelly pays for both books. At the cafe next door, we order lattes and coffee cake. It's unseasonably warm, so we sit outside.

I flip through my book and rest it on my lap. "Thank you for my gift. But tell me what's really going on."

Shelly delays her response by hiding behind her coffee cup.

I cross my arms and give her the stink eye.

She sets her cup down. "I have two things to tell you. One of which you're going to love."

"And the other one?

"Not so much."

I give her a lopsided grin and drink from my latte. "May as well spill it."

She stirs her drink. "I'll start with the good news. First off, you've known about your father for almost a year and it's time to connect with him."

"That's not for you to decide." Last summer, Shelly made me her pet project when I told her I'd never met my father. We spent weeks trying to find out the guy's identity, and discovered he lives in Seattle and writes bestsellers about climate change. The more I learn about him, the more I know I'm not worthy to claim myself as this guy's son.

"But I found a way to get you to Seattle."

I squint at her. "How?"

She pulls a white business envelope from her purse and hands it to me. It's addressed to me at her parents' address, and I notice the University of Washington return address. They already rejected me, so I'm confused. The letter reads, "Congratulations, Michael G. Flynn: You've been accepted into the Hugo House Summer of Writing Workshop." I look up. "What the hell? I never applied for this."

"I found it online and applied for you."

I frown and scan the letter again. "Why would you do something like that without asking?"

She shrugs. "We had to get you to Seattle so you could meet your dad. I figured it was worth a shot."

I fling the letter across the table. "Thanks, but no thanks."

"Michael, if you want to be a writer, you have to experience life outside of Rooster, Ohio."

"What if I want to write about Rooster?"

"Hemingway had to move to France in order to write about the Midwest, and he couldn't write about France until he came back to the states."

I slap the table. "I'm not Hemingway!" Our cups sway.

She places her palm against my forearm. "Neruda, you'll have a chance to improve your writing, *and* be in the same city as your father."

I chew on a cuticle. "This isn't what I planned after graduation." Okay, so I hadn't really planned anything. But still.

She hauls out her iPad and pulls up the site. "Look. It's three weeks, and you'll live in a dorm and take classes with other word nerds." She passes me her tablet.

I swipe through the page. "It costs almost three thousand bucks."

"You got a full scholarship."

I glance at the letter again. "Yeah, well, I'd still have to get there. The Whale eats gas, and I doubt it would make as far as Dayton."

"So, you'll fly there."

I furrow my brow. "Doesn't that require money?"

"We'll find a way, Neruda. Listen, this is meant to be. It's being handed to you."

I take a deep breath and scroll through the site again. "I had no idea stuff like this was out there."

"That's why you have me." She grins. "I'm your human Google."

"How *did* you get me in?"

"I filled out the application and clicked send."

I squint. "How'd you fill it out?"

"You used my laptop to write your college apps. Also, I sent one of your college application essays. You *do* write pretty well."

"For a redneck?"

She punches me lightly. "For anyone, silly."

I scratch my head. "How'd you pull off the teacher recommendations?"

"Duh. I emailed Mrs. Silver and Mrs. Tucker. They wrote glowing recommendations, and Mrs. Rhinehart sent them your transcripts and ACT scores. Plus, I had all your identification info from when we tried to find your birth certificate."

I set her iPad on the table. "Why do you want me to do this?"

"Because you don't grow unless you get out of your comfort zone."

"You live a leisurely lifestyle with your big house and pool," I say.

Shelly snatches her iPad off the table. "I'm not talking about furniture and swimming pools. I'm talking about stretching your brain. Besides, my life isn't all easy street."

"I know." I sling an arm around her and rest my cheek against hers. She's had her share of drama. "I'm sorry."

"I'm only forgiving you because you smell like melted butter and cinnamon."

I kiss the crown of her head. "But why didn't you tell me you did this?"

"I figured if you didn't get in, no problem, because you didn't know about it in the first place. But you got in, with a full scholarship."

I sit back and study her. To the uninformed observer, my girlfriend's straight, black ponytail and bangs over bright blue eyes make her look innocent. Little do they know. "Shelly, I've lived my whole life teetering on the edge. I've earned the right to rest and have a lazy ass summer. There comes a time in everyone's life when things should be unexciting."

"Yeah, when you're ninety." She fixes those baby blues on me. "There's more for you to do, Michael Neruda Flynn. You need to get out of Rooster and find out how the world works."

"I've done worldly stuff," I say. "I lived in my car for nearly a year, and I almost burned down the high school."

Shelly sighs. "That's not worldly stuff. Those are bad circumstances and stupid decisions. You have to go away for a while. There's stuff for you to do. One is to meet your father."

I've known Shelly long enough to suspect there's something else going on. "Why are you trying to get rid of me?"

She hesitates, and her voice gets tinny. "I'm not. I just want you to take advantage of this golden opportunity."

I chew on my cuticle again. "You said there were two things you had to tell me." I arch my eyebrows. "You haven't contacted my father, too, have you?"

"God, no," she says. "Even *I* have limits."

Neither of us speaks for a few moments. Then she says, "I've done everything I can to get you there. It's up to you to take the next step."

I slump in my chair. "I just don't want to end up being homeless again. Now that my sister and I have a decent place to live, I kind of want to stay here."

"The workshop is only three weeks. You can come back."

I look at the letter again. "I have until April tenth if I choose to accept."

She scowls at me. "What do you mean *if*? There's no *if*. You *are* going."

"Maybe. Maybe not."

She settles against my chest. "Think about it overnight?"

Her hair smells exotic, like ginger and nutmeg, and I almost want to take a bite out of her. "Okay, I'll mull it over." I reach for the Murakami and page through it. "So, what's the other horrible thing you did to me?"

She crosses her arms. "When you put it that way, I'm not sure I want to tell you."

"How much worse can it be?"

"I guess it depends on your perspective."

I sigh and set the paperback on the table. "Just tell me."

She squeezes her eyes shut and takes a deep breath. "I've been accepted to Goucher College in Baltimore, Maryland."

I draw back from her. "You applied out of *state*?"

"It's where my mom went to school."

"But it's out of state!"

"I never said I wanted to stay in Rooster. Or *Ohio* for that matter."

My chair scrapes the concrete as I shoot up. "I'm outta here." I head down the street toward where I parked her car.

Shelly retrieves my book and the letter and runs to catch up to me. "Neruda, did you really think I'd want to stay here?"

I stop and look at her. The girl who knows all my secrets and accepts me as I am. "Yeah. I thought you'd want to stay with me."

***

Shelly sits in the passenger side and clicks her seatbelt. As soon as I start the car I crank the music. Talking would be a bad idea right now.

Normally we take scenic roads back to Rooster from Columbus, but today I barrel east on I-70, jaw clenched, laser focused on the road. Shelly lets me silently stew as Coldplay screams from her car stereo.

I park Shelly's car in her driveway and shut off the ignition. I dump her keys on top of the dashboard. "See ya."

As I walk down the drive, I hear her say. "Michael, you forgot your book."

I give her a backhanded wave and don't stop. "Keep it."

"Michael, don't be that way."

The Whale's old engine makes a loud *phoomp* when I turn the key and pull away from her house.

Chapter Two

Shelly

Shelly trudges into her kitchen and plunks her purse and the two books on the counter. "Men!"

Her mom snaps a lid on a large salad bowl as she walks in. "You're home early."

"I told Michael about getting into Goucher."

Her mother sets the salad in the fridge. "And it didn't go well?"

Shelly shakes her head, knowing if she speaks it will come out all fractured and she'll have the ugly cry.

Mrs. Miller reaches for her daughter, and Shelly ends up sputtering into her mom's chest.

"Did you point out that Towson is only a six and half hour drive?"

"He didn't give me a chance."

Mrs. Miller caresses Shelly's hair. She lets her mom hold her for a bit. Then she pulls back and wipes her face with her palm. "I need a cigarette."

"How many have you had today?"

"It's only my third."

"I'm starting a yoga class just for people trying to quit smoking," she says. "You should join us."

Shelly rolls her eyes. "I'd be the only one there less than a hundred years-old."

Mrs. Miller grins. "Actually, there's a twenty-one-year-old in the class."

"Thanks, but no thanks, Mom." Shelly *is* trying to curb her nicotine habit, but on her own terms.

"Well, at least you're not stealing them anymore."

She gives her mom a sheepish grin. "How did you know about that?"

"Shelly, I'm not an idiot. I was raised with your mother."

"She stole cigarettes?"

Her mom wipes the counter near the sink with a sponge. "That, and more. She also found a way to 'earn' them."

Shelly blanches. Her birth mother, who is her mom's sister, disappeared when Shelly was a toddler. Most of her life she didn't know her mom and dad are actually her aunt and uncle. Two years ago, after she found out, something inside her split. Every single day Shelly regrets how she hurt them by running away. Even after all the shit Shelly put her parents through, they still love her and she wonders why. There's a wild animal inside her, one she didn't inherit from them, and Shelly struggles to restrain her impulses. "I'm sorry, Mom."

"Well, we've weathered a lot of storms together," Mrs. Miller says. "And I'm blaming Jack Kerouac."

Shelly sniffs a laugh. Other than smoking, Shelly stayed out of trouble, and for the most part, adapted to living in Rooster. Yet even in moments of great happiness, like eating cake with chocolate frosting or performing the perfect jump in cheerleading, Shelly always felt deep sorrow, as if she blinked, joy would evaporate and never return.

She's never shared this with her mom. It would break her heart, so Shelly buries her feelings.

During her sophomore year, Shelly fell in love with words when her English teacher quoted a few lines from *On the Road*. Her mom might believe Jack Kerouac ruined her life, but to Shelly, Kerouac tore off the bandages and exposed her slanted soul.

Shelly and Michael attend the same high school, but they never knew each other until their first day of community service. He hung around a group of nerds who spent their free time in the library, and she was a cheerleader, so their paths only crossed once.

The day Mrs. Silver read lines from *On the Road*, Shelly stopped in the library on her way to lunch to see if they had the book.

Michael sat at the circulation desk reading a book that may have been published when Abraham Lincoln was president. He glanced up, his eyes half hidden by dark, shaggy bangs. At the time Shelly thought he wasn't bad looking for a book nerd.

"Do you have *On the Road*, or any books by Jack Kerouac?" She asked.

He set his book down and searched on the library computer. "Nope."

In the hallway outside the library Shelly pulled the Amazon site up on her phone and ordered *On the Road*.

Until the book arrived in the mail, she remained regular old Shelly Miller, a cheerleader who wore her long blonde hair in a ponytail. But that girl was a lie.

Chapter Three
Michael

The drive back from Columbus cools my jets. Somewhat.

By the time I pull The Blue Whale, my 1982 Ford LTD station wagon, onto the gravel driveway at Earl and Dot's house, I'm less pissed. Earl, the high school custodian, supervised Shelly's and my community service last summer. When he discovered I was living in my car, he and his wife took my sister Annie and me in.

I wipe my feet on the door mat and hang The Whale's keys on the rack near the back door. Dot stands at the sink rinsing lettuce for salad. "Something smells awesome."

The wrinkles on Dot's face disappear as she smiles at me. "Dinner will be ready soon."

I saunter into the living room and plop onto the sofa next to my sister Annie. As usual, she's absorbed in a book.

"Holy crap, what a day." I mutter. Normally I'd use stronger language, but not within earshot of Dot or Earl.

Annie closes her book. "What's the matter?"

I run a hand through my hair. "Shelly applied for a writing workshop for me in Washington, and I got in."

"The state of Washington? Or DC?"

"The state."

"Holy crap is right," she says. "How will you pay for it?"

"They offered me a full scholarship"

"That's awesome, Michael."

"But it's in freaking Seattle."

"Wait! Isn't that where your dad lives?"

"Bingo." I slump into the cushions, and extend my legs like a spider. "But Shelly did this all behind my back. *Plus,* she told me she's going to college in Maryland. It's like she's trying to get rid of me."

Annie leans against me. "I guess you *have* had a crappy day."

***

After dinner, I work at the movie theatre, and it's a busy night, so for a few hours I can forget about my future, or lack of it. When I get home, I look up the University of Washington web page and find the link to the writing workshop.

The three-week intensive HHSOW (Hugo House Summer of Writing) is a dynamic, creative opportunity for recent high school graduates who intend to pursue writing and related careers. Located on the University of Washington campus in the heart of Seattle, students will reside in the famed university district...

The videos and photos from past workshops reveal a tree lined campus and walking/biking trails. Something about this workshop feels right, like if I don't do this, the path not taken will be me spending the next sixty years merely existing in Rooster, Ohio. And this might be my only chance to meet my father.

Shelly, what have you done to me?

Exercise helps me think, so I drop to the floor and do pushups. I reach a hundred and collapse onto my back. As I lie there, sweaty and gasping for air, a stink bug crawls up the wall. "What should I do, Mr. Stink Bug? I'm afraid to stay here, yet scared to leave."

Annie has a safe, loving home now, so I can stop worrying about her. My brother Jeff, lives with his dad Paul.

But then there's our mom.

Whether I stay or go, her problems won't disappear.

Chapter Four
Michael

After Biology class at the college, I have a little time before work, so I stop to see Paul, my brother's father. He's the closest thing I've had to a father all my life.

Paul's garage is a combination junk yard and car fix-up place. Patsy Cline sings, "Walkin' After Midnight" in the background. Paul stands at the counter, writing in a receipt book as he mumble-hums the song. He looks up and smiles. "Hey, Michael. How are those tires working out?"

"Great." Paul had sold me four reconditioned tires last summer for fifty bucks. Later, I looked up the cost and found out he had practically given them to me. "They got me through winter."

Paul sets aside his receipt book. "What can I do for you for today?"

I glance into the garage and notice a couple of his guys working under a Ford Taurus on the lift. "You busy?"

"I can spare a few minutes," Paul says. He walks over to the soda case and pulls out a *7Up*. "You thirsty?"

"Sure. I'll take a Coke."

He fishes around and hands me a can.

"Thanks."

"It's a nice day," Paul says. "Let's go take a walk in the garden."

His garden is heaps of old cars. Some are crushed, stacked like metal pancakes, waiting to be melted down. Others are models he keeps to sell for parts. He gets a lot of guys who restore old cars and need a quarter panel for a '67 Mustang, or guys like me who drive pieces of junk and need to keep them running.

There's a clear gravel path between piles of junkers. Paul stops and takes a deep breath. "Time to stop and smell the scrap metal."

I laugh. There *is* something peaceful about all these ravaged cars. It's like an enormous sculpture.

"I come out here and think when I'm troubled," he says.

"What makes you think I'm troubled?"

Paul grins. "It's all over your face, kid. You'd make a lousy poker player."

I sigh and take a drink of Coke. "Yeah, I have a few issues."

"Girl trouble?"

"No, Shelly and I are fine." I'm still pissed off at her, but one problem at a time. "But I've sort of opened Pandora's box."

"What do you mean?"

I drink more pop. The burn on my throat calms me. "I know who my father is."

"Whoa." Paul takes a giant gulp of *7Up* and wipes his mouth with the back of his hand. "Did Susan finally tell you?"

"No, and she doesn't know that I know. "

"How'd you find out?"

"Remember last summer when I worked at the school for my community service?" Paul nods, and I continue. "Well, that's how I met Shelly. And when I told her I didn't know who my father was, she made it her goal to help me find out. And in our search, we discovered Mom's old diary from her senior year."

Paul drops his chin. "You took Shelly inside Susan's house?"

"I didn't want to, but Mom refused to tell me his identity. So, Shelly, Annie, and I started poking around."

Paul shakes his head and guzzles the rest of his pop. He lobs the empty can at the unrolled window of a rusted '72 Buick Skylark. "What did you find out?"

"It wasn't easy," I say. "She had crossed out his name on every entry, but we used some of the details to scrounge old yearbooks and figure it out." I look at Paul. "Nice mullet you had, by the way."

He laughs, and scratches at the remaining hair on the back of his head. "So, who is he?"

"Ashton Meadows."

Paul nods, and I sense he's known all along. "Have you told Susan you figured it out?"

"No. I don't know how to, or even if I should."

We stop walking. Paul rests his hand on my shoulder. "She might have enough on her plate right now with the threat of eviction."

I shudder.

We resume walking. "What do you plan to do about your father?" Paul asks.

"He's a professor at University of Washington, which is one of the schools where I applied. They turned me down, but I got accepted into this summer writing workshop in Seattle. It's all paid for, and I think I may go."

"Good for you! Congratulations."

"Yeah, but I'd be away from Mom for almost a month. Even though she's still not speaking to me, I'm here if anything happens and she needs me."

"Don't worry about Susan," Paul says. "She can always come to me for help."

"But that's the thing. She won't *go* to anyone for help. She thinks she's fine."

"Your mother and I have a long history. I'll take care of her."

"But what about Dee Dee?" Paul's wife hates his association with me and my mother. She tolerates Jeff since he's Paul's son. Mom and I are another story.

"Dee Dee knows I have responsibilities," he says. We walk a few yards. "You said two things troubled you."

I finish off my Coke, but I hold onto the can. "I don't think my father knows he's my father."

Paul nods. "Yeah, I doubt he knows. Your mom never told me, either."

"But you knew."

"I sort of figured it out. She and I broke up halfway through senior year. She spent a lot of time with Meadows, and I knew she kind of liked him." He glances at me. "And you grew up to look just like him. But it wasn't my place to tell you."

"How well did you know my father?"

"Not well at all. He was in a different social class, and he hung around other jocks and smart kids." He smirks. "Kids like me didn't mix with kids like him."

I look down and kick at chunks of gravel.

"I'm sorry, Michael. I wish I could tell you more," Paul says. "He seemed like a decent guy." We walk in silence for a few beats. "His girlfriend, though." He shook his head. "I knew *her*. She used to torment your mother."

"Ellie?"

"Yeah. How did you know that?"

"The diary."

"Right." He tightens his lips. "I remember one time we were walking down the hall. Ellie and her posse started complaining of a bad smell as soon we passed them." He looks at me. "Back then your mom was very clean, and she worked hard not to look like a poor kid."

"Whatever happened to Ellie?"

"She still lives in town." Paul stops. "You're not thinking of talking to Ellie Carson about your dad, are you?"

"No, I don't think she'll give me an objective opinion."

"Are you planning to meet your father while you're in Seattle?"

"I don't know. I'm pretty sure he's married and has a family. Me just showing up out of nowhere may cause a lot of trouble."

Paul nods. "What do you know about him?"

"He's a semi-famous marine biologist who specializes in sea turtles."

"Cool. Does he travel to the Galapagos Islands and stuff?"

"Yeah, and he did a TED talk about underwater life."

We walk a few more paces toward Paul's office. "Have you thought of how you'll approach him if you decide to meet him?" he asks.

"I have no idea."

Paul considers this. "Do you want me to contact him?"

"That would make life easier. But my gut tells me this should be between him and me." I follow Paul into the office and toss my empty pop can in the trash. Patsy Cline sings, "Heartache." "Should I even bother? I mean, maybe this is a secret I should keep to myself."

Paul steps behind the counter. "If I had a long-lost son out there, I'd sure want to know."

Chapter Five

April 4
Michael

I text Shelly.

-Meet me in library before your next class.

The sight of her strolling toward me makes my insides flicker. I've missed her. Missed us skin to skin, febrile and cool, her soft curves pliable against my rigid bones. I glance away to cool my thoughts.

She sits down and dumps her bag on the table. "Your face is all red."

"Is it?"

The student worker dude at the desk glowers at us. He went to Rooster High last year, so maybe he believes all the rumors about us. When Shelly ran off, people gossiped she had joined a cult or had become a prostitute. She did run away, but to search for her birth mother.

The rumors about me were true; I *did* go to jail before I was assigned community service.

Shelly kisses me. "So, are you and I okay?"

I shrug. "I guess."

"I really think this writing class is the best thing for you."

I squeeze her hand. "I know you do."

The library staff isn't friendly, but their calico cat Sugar slinks out to rub against our legs. Shelly scratches behind Sugar's ears, and the cat moves on to another table.

"I met with Paul yesterday," I say. "He thinks I should contact my father."

Shelly wrinkles her brow. "Were you thinking of *not* contacting him? We went to a lot of trouble to find the guy."

The afternoon Shelly, Annie, and I crawled around my mother's disaster of a house, searching for my birth certificate we all should have worn Hazmat suits. So she's right on that score. "I don't want to screw up his life," I say.

"How do you know his life isn't already a mess?"

"You saw him on his TED talk. He seems normal."

"That's his public face," she says. "He might keep his wife and kids chained up in the basement."

I pull a notebook and pen out of my bag. "I don't think he'd have his job if he did."

Shelly crosses her arms and scowls. "You're thinking of going all the way there and not even *calling* the guy?"

I shrug.

She pulls her laptop out of her book bag and opens the faculty page on the University of Washington website. Beneath a picture of my father, who resembles an older, smarter version of me, is a phone number and an email address, along with a link to his university web page. Shelly slides her computer over to me.

I give her a panicky look. "I can't do it right now. I have to mull this over."

"But you can copy the information down."

I groan and scrawl the email and phone number down in my notebook. I flip to a fresh page. Shelly picks up her history textbook and opens it. "I envy you," I say. "You just need to read about a bunch of crap that happened eons ago, not open a ginormous can of worms."

"Seriously, Neruda? You know I hate when you get all whiny."

"It's part of my charm." I chew on the end of my pen. If only there were instruction manuals on how to write to the father who doesn't know you exist. I start writing.

Dear Dr. Meadows.

My mother and you were classmates at Rooster High about twenty years ago.

~~You humped against the side of the building at homecoming and did her under the stage on Valentine's Day. The whole time you were screwing my mother you ignored her, like she was cheap trash, and slinked around with your preppy girlfriend Ellie, whose son, by the way, bullies my sister. But that's another story.~~

You may not know it, but you're my father.

~~I'm the baby that came out of you banging her in the prop room, and If you DID know she was having your baby but left anyway then you're a real shit heel because her life turned into a mess. Literally. She hoards every piece of junk that comes into her house. I'm part of the fallout she holds on to because you left. So fuck you.~~

~~Maybe you're not the sole reason she's crazy and you may not even know it, but my mother is freaking nuts and your sperm didn't help matters and it looks like things turned out well for you so kiss my ass and~~

~~FUCKYOUFUCKYOUFUCKFUCKFUCK~~

Shelly glances at me over her book. "How's it going?"

"Just great." I set my pen down, grasp my hair by the roots and growl. Sugar leaps onto the table and settles herself on top of my notebook. The cat stares up at me.

"Problem solved," Shelly says. "The cat has decided now is not the time."

I give Shelly a thin smile and scratch the top of Sugar's head. "I'm really angry at him, and I don't know where it's coming from."

She rubs a hand down my back. "Do you blame him for how things turned out for your mom?"

"Partly, yeah. I mean, he might *not* know about me, but if he does, that changes the stakes in our potential for having a relationship."

Shelly considers this. "Do you think he *does* know about you?"

The cat purrs under my fingers as I stroke its chin. "Paul says there wasn't time or opportunity for Mom to tell him."

Sugar has had enough of me and jumps off the table. I rip the scribbled sheet from my notebook and wad it up. "But I resent the way Ashton Meadows carried on with my mom secretly. Like she was a nice piece of ass, but not good enough for him to be *seen* with. So yeah, I kind of hate him for that."

I unfold the letter and look it over. "This sucks." I rip it into small pieces.

Shelly curls herself against me and leans her head on my shoulder. "You don't need to write the letter today."

***

After classes, Shelly and I sit in her bedroom, staring at her computer screen. My hand hovers over the keypad. All I have to do is click *Accept*.

"What are you waiting for?"

I sit back in the chair and look at her. "What if I'm the worst writer there?"

She forms a moustache with a lock of her black, dyed hair. "That's the chance you'll have to take."

I reach into my side pocket, pull out a tube of antacids, and pop a couple in my mouth.

"You've been eating a lot of those lately," she says.

"You keep giving give me reasons to."

She sticks her tongue out and crosses her eyes. "If you don't attend this workshop you'll hate yourself forever."

I frown at her. "You don't think you'll miss me? Once you leave for college you'll never see me again."

"So maudlin, Neruda." She releases the lock of hair. "I'll be in Maui with my folks during the workshop, anyway."

I knock the side of my head with my pencil. "But I won't know anyone there."

"You'll be with other word nerds. Maybe you'll even meet one who lived in their car."

I snort. "Did I mention I hate you?" I close my eyes and click *Accept*.

Shelly throws her arms around me and squeezes. "You'll finally get to meet your dad!"

I cross my arms. "For all I know he'll be off tagging sea turtles in the Galapagos or studying coral reefs in Bora Bora."

"In any case, you'll get out of Rooster for a while."

"What if I hate Seattle?"

"Theo loves it there." Shelly's eyes get big and she slaps her thighs. "Wait! I'll fly out with you on my way to Hawaii, and you and I can stay with Theo for a few days before you move into the dorm."

I sputter a laugh. "You want your *current* boyfriend to stay with your *ex*-boyfriend?"

She waves like she's swiping left. "He's past history. Besides, he has a girlfriend." She wraps her hands around my bicep. "It'll be fun. What's the worst that can happen?"

I arch my eyebrows. "I can think of a thousand and one things."

"That's because you have an overactive imagination."

"And you're sure Theo won't mind?"

"He'll love it. Look. I'll even text him and ask." She whips out her phone and texts.

"What if he doesn't get back to you until after we get there and we're walking the streets trying to find…"

Shelly's phone buzzes and she shows me the screen. *-Sure. ☺ Just let me know when.* "See? Problem solved."

This is such a bad idea, but once Shelly fixates on something there's no way around it, so I say, "Okay."

"Now let's make plane reservations."

I feel my stomach clench. "I don't know how."

"It's easy." She scoots closer to me and opens a tab on her browser. "First you get on Orbitz and compare prices. What day do you want to leave?"

They said I should be there by June seventh."

"Let's go on the fifth and spend a couple of days before hand bumming around Seattle. That gives us Wednesday, Thursday, and most of Friday before you move into the dorm."

Shelly types and the screen fills up with several pages of options.

I stare at the screen. "It all looks like hieroglyphics. Shouldn't I know how to do this kind of thing?"

"Why would you?" she says. "You've never traveled."

"There's so much I *don't* know."

"Which is why you need to do this workshop."

I hate when she's right.

Shelly finds a flight through Los Angeles that will put us in Seattle around noon. "Should I book it?"

"This is way out of my comfort zone." I squeeze my eyes shut. "Do it."

Shelly pulls out her credit card and pays for the flights. She claps. "It's official. You're going to Seattle!"

I eat a couple more antacids.

She tugs at my sleeve. "Come on, you. I'm hungry. Let's go downstairs and raid the refrigerator."

We fix turkey sandwiches, grab a bag of Cheetos, and sit on the red leather couch in the her tricked-out family room. A rerun of Shelly's favorite show, *The Big Bang Theory*, is on.

"Haven't you seen every episode about forty-seven times?" I say.

She bundles her feet under her butt. "Yeah, but it's funny."

I shake my head. "It's like dating a monkey."

She poses like and ape and grunts.

"The gorilla my dreams." I chomp on my sandwich. "By the way, do you want to go to prom next week?"

She scrunches her face. "No *freaking* way!"

I do a fist pump in the air. "Thank you. You've made me the happiest man alive."

"Given what happened last year," she says, "they'd probably throw you out. There's a wanted poster of you in the hallway."

I grab a handful of *Cheetos*. "Yeah, it's hanging right next to yours."

As we eat, I study the framed family portrait above the mantle. "You look like the kind of blonde family you'd see in a frame at Wal Mart."

"Ugh. That blonde girl in the photo is a total freak."

The family photo was taken shortly before Shelly found out her brother Josh is actually her cousin, and her parents are technically her aunt and uncle.

I run my fingers through Shelly's dyed hair. "I like the black. It's like you're wearing midnight on your head." I start plaiting some of her long strands.

"Are you getting Cheeto dust in my hair?"

"Yes. I'm braiding it in."

"When did you learn to braid?" she asks.

"I used to do Annie's hair when we were kids. I'm pretty good at it."

Shelly gawks at the TV as I weave my fingers through her strands. She jabs me in the ribs with one of her knife-sharp elbows. "You're a terrible boyfriend, you know."

"Why? I just asked you to the prom. You said no." I let go of her braid and it unspools in loose waves.

She gestures to the screen. "Wolowitz just wrote Bernadette a love song. You never do stuff like that for me."

I run my fingers through her hair again and weave a new braid. "What are you talking about? I quote Neruda to you all the time. You even named me after him." This time I clamp her hair with a paper clip.

"You're always scribbling stuff down in your little notebooks, yet you've never once written me a love poem."

"Neruda says it better than I ever could. Besides, I'm not a poet."

"Then write me a story,"

I scrunch my face. "I don't write about people I care about. I just make shit up." I kiss the top of her head. "Why don't *you* write *me* a poem?"

Shelly sits up and gazes at me. "There once was a cretin named Michael, whose body was quite an eyeful…" I flex my arms for her. "But he lived in his car, and he couldn't go far because the gas tank would not stay full."

I clutch my chest, feigning emotional ecstasy. "Your words stir such deep feelings in me."

She flicks the braid at me and sits on top of my outstretched legs. "Okay, now *you* write a story about me."

I cup her cheeks in my hands and pretend to study her face. "She has eyes the color of a filthy swimming pool, lips as bright as rotting blood oranges on a humid day, and a voice that could break nails."

"She sounds divine," Shelly upturns her chin and pouts her lips. "What's this delicious creature's name?"

"Simone. Simone le Fever."

"Tell me more," Shelly gushes.

"Simone thrusts her six-foot-seven, five-hundred-pound frame against the ridiculously handsome Prince Flynnstone of Mikelandia. Prince Flynnstone, aghast, tries to run from her clutches, but she ensnares him within her arms, which turn to snakelike rubber, and she ties herself around his body. She knots him with her long, black tresses, kissing the oxygen right out of him until he stops breathing, yet he dies happily ever after."

"Oh, baby, that's so hot," she says, in a husky voice. "it's almost as good as a Pelee Peugeot novel." She collapses on me and plants kisses all over my face. "Tell me more."

I hold one of her hands. "Naked, your skin is like that of a Gila Monster, your hands as soft as meat cleavers, and your eyes as bright as sewer water."

Shelly wraps her arms around my neck. "I think we need to take this up to my room where I can suffocate you slowly with my tentacles."

***

Later, I pick Annie up from after band practice. I tell her about booking my flight.

"I think it's cool that you're going to Seattle," she says. "You get to try on a new city. Maybe you'll find it fits better than Rooster."

I snort. "You make it sound like I'm trying on clothes."

"It sort of is," she says. "Rooster's always been too tight for you."

"How about you? Does Rooster fit?"

Annie crosses her arms. "After going to the New York trip with the band, Rooster feels like shoes giving me blisters."

I look at Annie. "So, what do you want to do with your life?"

She shrugs. "I don't know. But I can get scholarships by pulling the mixed-race, poverty stricken, foster child, Appalachian cards."

I snicker. "Do you have somewhere in mind?"

She leans her head back against the seat. "No. Just somewhere away from here. Away from Mom."

"Even if Mom cleans her place up?"

"She's never going to clean that shit up." Annie looks out the window and doesn't speak for a long time. "I think I'm done with Mom."

"But she's our mother."

"She doesn't care about us, Michael. All she cares about are her mounds of junk." Annie runs her hands over her thighs, and picks at a loose thread on a hole in her jeans. "She doesn't talk to us anymore anyway. We may as well be orphans."

In a way Annie *is* an orphan. Her father died when she was three and Mom's a whack job. Of all the kids in the family, Annie pulled the shortest straw.

"I want to get far away from here," she says. "Find new friends, marry a guy from a big, normal family, and make sure my children never, ever resort to living in their cars."

"It wasn't all bad," I say. "Except when it snowed or stormed. But hey, you lived on the back porch. How did you handle bad weather?"

"Ugh." She wraps her arms around herself. "I went inside. I slept in a folding chair where I could find space. I doused myself with baby powder to mask the odor and slept under a sheet."

I shake my head. "We've had one freaky ass childhood, haven't we?"

"Yeah. I'm so grateful to Dot and Earl for rescuing us."

"Same here."

She reaches over and hugs my shoulder. "I'm glad you and Jeff are my brothers. Things would have been worse if you guys were jerks."

Chapter Six

Late April
Michael

Me-*Don't forget to bring homework for our prom night!!
Thrills!* I text to Shelly.

Shelly-*Xciting!* Shelly replies.

Me-*Loaded my Starbux card with 20$. Go wild.*

Shelly-*So romantic*

Me-*U can order a latte. & a pastry.*

Shelly-*This will B the prom of my dreams.*

Me-*Am I the world's best boyfriend, or what?"*

Shelly-*You're better than nothing.*

Me-*Gee. thanks.* ☹

Me-*I shall pick you up in my chariot in 15.*

Me-*Prepare to be amazed.*

I always park on the street to avoid leaving oil stains on her parents' custom driveway. I may be a juvenile delinquent, but I'm the most conscientious one you'll ever meet.

Shelly stands on the driveway wearing skinny jeans and a Jack Kerouac T-shirt. She smiles when she notices my tuxedo T-shirt. "Nice shirt."

I stop to pose in the driveway. "Designed by Walmart."

"We make a startlingly fashionable couple," she says.

"We do, don't we?"

As she and I snap a couple of selfies, her mom comes out of the house. "Let me at least take a couple of pictures of you goofballs." We hand her our phones. "You're really just going to Starbucks and not the prom?"

"I'm so over high school, Mom." Shelly elbows me. "And this guy's on the no-fly list at school."

I take a bow. "I bid you good night, Mrs. Miller." I gaze at Shelly. "Your chariot awaits, mademoiselle." We link arms and promenade down to The Blue Whale.

Mrs. Miller follows and snaps a photo of the two of us standing in front of the giant blue station wagon. "Be careful and have fun," she says.

***

As we pull into the Starbuck's lot, Shelly and I notice a few Rooster High students dressed in prom gear carrying drinks. Some kids cast us furtive glances, but most just ignore us.

We find a table near the back, dump our bags, and order lattes and muffins.

Shelly starts reading from *Norwegian Wood* by Haruki Murakami, and I sort through the stack of index cards I created for my Biology final.

"I tried writing another letter to my father last night but they keep coming out as poems," I say.

She sets her book down. "Read them to me."

"They're pretty raw." I grab my notebook from my pack and page through its. I clear my throat. "This one's called Dear Dad."

Dear Dad
Sometimes I want to kill you before I've even met you.
Beat you senseless
The way you left my mother, defenseless.

I'd like to crumple you like a used paper towel
the way you disposed of Mom like she was foul.
I'd hide your body in a dark room under the stage
You liked her just fine as long as she kept out of range,
By daylight she was just some girl you tutored in
science.
Sometimes I just want to kill you, you sonofabitch.

"It sounds like a rap song," Shelly says.
"Just call me P Mikey."
"You're really pissed off at him, aren't you?"
"I'm getting slightly less pissed as I write, but yeah, kind of."
"Read the next one."
"Okay. I don't have a title for it yet."

I'm the canary the cat swallowed.
Did you know you planted seeds for a dandelion?
Or was she just a piece of candy that lost its flavor
after too many bites?

I'll bet she dreamed of wearing a white lace dress for
you
but she wore brown polyester and served you burgers
and fries
while your girlfriend muttered lies about my mother.
You treated my mother like a queen inside the fairy
tale room
full of stage props, deep inside the belly of the school,
But in the brightly lit hallways she was a mirage.

My mother could have been anything if it weren't for us.
You and your insistent sex
Me, your progeny.
We ruined her, you AND i.
So here's the thing. You're my father.
I'll be in town if you want to meet me.

I set my notebook down. "Like I said, I haven't earned the name Neruda."

Shelly rests her chin on her hand. "Do you really blame yourself for being born? It's not like you could help it."

"No, I blame him, mostly. But I didn't make things easier for her."

"Michael, you can't blame yourself for your mom's psychosis. It was a confluence of tragedies."

I rest my elbows on the table and lean in. "Confluence. That's a perfect word for it."

"Sounds like something *you'd* say, Mr. AP English. I've clearly been hanging around you too long." She takes a sip of her latte. "My next boyfriend will be much dumber."

"What's *that* supposed to mean?"

"I'm kidding."

"No, you're not. You're already planning your next out-of-state boyfriend at your out-of-state college."

She drapes her arms around my shoulders and tries to kiss me but I jerk away. "Really? You're going to be *that* guy? She picks up her book again. "Sometimes you can be a giant cactus, Neruda, but you're not a dandelion."

Chapter Seven
Early May
Michael

Shelly and I lie head to head in the sun on the concrete next to her parents' pool. The water is a day or two away from being warm enough for swimming, but baking in the sun all day has rendered the cement pleasantly warm. Shelly thought lying on concrete is a sensation we should explore.

"I wouldn't call this comfortable," I say.

She stretches and dangles her hands above my face. "It's practice for when I lie on the beach in Hawaii in a few weeks."

"Your life is so fucking hard." I bite at her fingers.

She giggles and picks up her book. We take turns reading passages aloud to one another from *Norwegian Wood.* I'm a couple of chapters ahead of her. "It's not Midori who's a patient in the hospital. It's…."

She bonks me with her book. "Stop giving me spoilers!"

I laugh. "You so remind me of Midori. "

"But she's so quirky."

"Exactly."

We read silently, and then I say, "so have you figured out what you're going to major in? At that college in another state that you didn't tell me you were applying to?"

She places her book face down on the ground. "I'm interested in everything, and not particularly good at anything. But I don't have to declare a major until the end of sophomore year."

I groan and sit up. "This cement is leaving imprints on my back."

"Wimp."

"I used to sleep in my car. I've earned the right *not* to rest on a bed of nails." I plunk onto a cushioned lawn chair. "Ahhhh, this is more like it."

Shelly plops down on the adjacent chair. The concrete has dotted the back of her thighs and calves like a popcorn ceiling. "I'm only moving so I can hear you better."

"Sure you are." I open my book. "Let's see what Japanese Shelly does next."

She swats me with her book again, bending the cover slightly. "Now you made me lose my place!"

I laugh. "Oh, so it's my fault you hit me?"

She flips through her copy to find where she left off and dog ears the page.

I cringe. "Books have feelings, you know."

She rolls her eyes. "You're such a freak you could join a circus."

"Ha ha. Maybe you should go into business management since you're good at running *my* life."

"Too boring. I want a vibrant, colorful career with my name in lights."

"Like movie star or rock star?"

"Now you're talking."

I mark my spot with a note card and roll to face her. "I think both of those require some sort of talent."

"There are plenty of people out there who are famous for being famous. I only need to figure out what will get me noticed."

I slide in next to her on her lounge chair. "I have no doubt you will find a way."

She rests her head against my chest. "We should have had a reality show when we did community service together. You'd be the guy famous for living in his car, and I'd be the girl who swooped in to rescue him."

"I'm glad we didn't. I'd like to forget the whole thing."

"All of it?"

"Well, maybe not *all* of it." I draw little circles on her arm with my fingertips and work down to her thigh. "I'd like to remember the dirty parts."

***

It's dinner time when I get home. After meat loaf, green beans, and mashed potatoes, Dot serves up fresh strawberry ice cream for dessert. Earl looks at me, and says, "let's go out on the porch, kid."

Whenever Earl wants a private talk, I get the feeling I'm in trouble. Maybe because Earl doesn't talk all that much. He just grumbles or yells.

We step outside with our bowls of ice cream. Earl sits in a rocker, and I face him by leaning against the railing.

Earl stretches his legs, rests his bowl on his chest, and loads his spoon. "This is a big trip for you."

I nod, my mouth filled with strawberry ice cream.

"First time out of state?"

"Yes, sir."

"First trip away from home is the hardest." Earl gazes out on the horizon. "I was about your age when I shipped off to Nam. Scared me shitless."

"Well yeah. You could have been killed."

"It wasn't just that," he says. "I knew I was not going to be the same when I came home. I'd see stuff that would change me. I worried that Dot would find someone else, and my father would find someone better to help him run things here at the farm. And yes, I also worried about dying." He stops to shovel in a couple of bites.

"But sometimes a man has to leave home to find himself. You're safe here. You know when you wake up, today is going to be just like yesterday and tomorrow. But you don't truly value that security until you go away and face a little danger." Earl sets his empty bowl on the floor.

"You might go out in the world and decide you like it better out there, and never come back. We see a lot of that these days because there's not much for young people here in Rooster. Lots of you kids are moving to Columbus and Cleveland or anywhere else to find work and excitement.

"But when you get out there, you might decide the world's just too crazy." He eyes me. "I want you to know you always have a place here with me and Dot."

"Thank you, sir. I'm grateful for everything you've done for me and Annie."

Earl groans like a bear as he stands. "Well, that's enough sentimental talk for me." He leans down to pick up his dish. "See you inside, kid."

I nod, and finish my dessert while scoping out the landscape. Myrna and Joy, the hens, tip through the yard on their chicken feet, and Bucky the rooster follows. Bucky is our alarm clock. "The girls" as Dot calls them, provide breakfast. They're so productive Earl takes eggs into school to give to Hess and the other custodians. They are the best eggs I've ever tasted.

Funny how you can feel close to a place that you've only lived in a few months. It would be easy to call this home. A lot of guys my age can't wait to tear out of town their first chance. I'm content here, yet soon my life will turn upside down.

Chapter Eight

May 26
Michael

On graduation day, Shelly and I meet for breakfast. The morning is sunny. "I thought milestones were always accompanied by rain," I say. "You know, to symbolize our transformations."

"That's only if you're in a story," Shelly says. "In real life, the weather does not cooperate with the plot."

Shelly's hair is tied up in a ragged knot and she's not wearing make-up, yet this is when I find her most beautiful.

"I'll take The Farmer's Breakfast," I tell the waitress. It includes three eggs, bacon, sausage, biscuits, and hash browns.

"Are you plowing a field later?" Shelly asks. "Don't forget we have party food to save room for."

I tell the waitress, "change that to the Sunrise with whole wheat toast." Shelly orders the same.

Shelly reaches into her bag, pulls out an envelope, and hands it to me. "Your graduation gift."

I slide my finger under the flap and pull out a note in my own handwriting. It reads: *IOU for plane fare.* The dollar amounts are scratched out and the balance is zero. "But I still owe you three hundred bucks."

"Not according to this." She taps at the signature line where her father has signed. "It's even witnessed by an attorney."

"Shelly, I can't accept this."

She waves it off. "It's a gift from my parents and me collectively." She takes my hand. "You need the money more than we do."

"Now I feel like a cheapskate for what I got you."

She rubs her palms together. "Gimme gimme."

"It's in the car," I mumble, and slouch out of my seat. I retrieve a large, thin package from the back seat.

Shelly tears the wrapping off to reveal a framed poster of the original paperback cover of *On the Road*. "I love it! It's so cool!"

"The sassy girl on the cover kind of reminds me of you. She has your no-shit attitude."

Shelly slides onto my lap and enfolds me in a bear hug. "It's perfect. I love it. Thank you, thank you, thank you."

At noon I walk into Shelly's three-car garage, which is filled with tables and chairs for her grad party.

The kitchen counters are laden with large deli trays of cheese, meat, fruit and vegetables. In the dining room, silver trays with burners underneath hold hot food. A woman wearing a name tag and a chef's uniform stirs one of the hot dishes. Stacks of plates, silverware, and glasses sit next to the hot food.

Shelly rushes up and kisses me. Standing outside by the pool I notice a guy I recognize from the family photos: her brother Josh. "Come on out, and I'll introduce you."

"Does he know half his wardrobe is missing?" I look down. I'm wearing a pair of Josh's khaki pants. Last year when Josh was studying in Europe, Shelly gave me a bunch of her brother's clothing. And now that he's at college in Boston, she still slips me shirts and pants. Sometimes they still have the store tags on them.

"He never noticed." We step outside. "Hey, Josh. This is the infamous Michael."

"Hey." He extends his hand. "Nice to meet you, even though you have really bad taste in women."

I laugh, and shake his hand. "She sort of chose me."

"She does that," he says.

The patio is crowded. "How many people are coming?"

"About a hundred or so," Shelly says.

"Do you even know a hundred people?"

"When Mom and Dad throw parties, they go all out," Josh says.

A little after two in the afternoon, Shelly finds me. "Let's get out of here. I can only stand to be polite to my parents' friends for so long."

The patchy front lawn at my brother's house looks like a used car lot with cars parked haphazardly. Scattered about on the grass are an assortment of bright plastic toys. A stuffed monkey dangles from one of the shrubs. "To say Jeff's party is a one-hundred-and-eighty-degree contrast from yours is an understatement," I say, as we walk toward the house.

"No kidding," Shelly mutters.

A collection of mis-matched chairs are scattered on the gravel driveway. "It's BYOC here-- Bring Your Own Chair."

The long table in the garage is full of food--potluck style. Paul stands at the grill cooking burgers and hot dogs. He's wearing a Sponge Bob hat and a *Kiss the Cook* apron. Charred hotdogs and burgers sit on a Styrofoam plate next to cheese slices wrapped in plastic. "Hey, Paul," I say.

"Hey, guys! Help yourselves to some eats."

I've already eaten a ton of food, but I grab a paper plate and fix a burger, and add potato chips and celery sticks.

Shelly leans in. "Aren't you glad you didn't pig out on the farmer's breakfast?" I hate when she's right.

"Jeff's out back," Paul says. "And hey, could you take these with you?" He hands me the plate of burgers and dogs. He gives Shelly bags of hot dog and hamburger buns.

Along the side of the house two teams are playing corn hole. Shelly leans against me. "I always thought the term corn hole sounded dirty."

"I know, right?"

We slip past the corn hole players to the back. Amid the dandelions and thistle, the back yard is slightly greener than the front, but it, too, is littered with assorted chairs and kids' toys. Loud country music emanates from someone's car stereo in the alley. I wonder if Shelly realizes *this* is how most kids in Rooster live.

I look around. "I hope my mom shows up."

"I'm looking forward to finally meeting her," Shelly says.

Shelly's been inside my mom's house, but I never took her back after we found Mom's journal. I haven't been there lately, either.

Jeff crosses the lawn to greet us. "I was worried you guys wouldn't come."

"Sorry," Michael says. "Got waylaid at Shelly's."

Jeff slings an arm around my shoulder. We're both six feet tall, but the resemblance ends there. Jeff is blonde and pale against my darkness.

"Well big Bro," Jeff says. "In a little over three hours we will both be high school graduates. We have to act like adults now."

"Doesn't mean we can't still be stupid." I put my brother in a head lock.

Jeff laughs, and squirms away. "Hey, did you see the cake?" A large frosted sheet cake dominates the table by the back door. "It's half white and half chocolate," Jeff says. "The chocolate side is yours since you're the black sheep of the family."

I bark a laugh. "I wonder whose idea that was."

Shelly pours warm pop in a plastic cup. "Is there any icc?"

"I'll get you some," I snatch the empty ice bucket and she follows me into the house. As I dig for ice in the cooler, I hear Paul in the living room. "I wish Susan would show up. Jeff was really looking forward to seeing her."

"She's probably too busy shopping at a yard sale to bother with her kids," his wife Dee Dee says. "That house is a pigsty. I'm surprised Children's Services didn't take her kids a long time ago."

Shelly gasps, and I storm past her into the living room holding the bucket. "Dee Dee, you can say whatever the *hell* you want about me but you do *not* get to talk about my mother!" I hurl the bucket across the room, and ice cubes clatter over the hardwood floor.

I back towards the front door. "I'm sorry, Paul, but I can't stay here." Paul gives me a resigned wave as I slam out.

Shelly finds me sitting in The Whale. "That was intense."

I smack the steering wheel. "Even if what she said is true, she doesn't have the right to say it."

"I'm sorry, Neruda." Shelly reaches for me. "Do you want to go back to my house?"

I gnaw on my cuticle. "I think I'm peopled out."

She leans against my shoulder. "Let's stop by the high school and see if our ducks are still in the pond."

I start the car. "I haven't been back there since last summer."

"Me, neither."

When we enter the school grounds, Shelly says, "The building's still standing."

"In spite of my lame attempt to blow it up?" I park The Whale next to Earl's truck. "What's Earl doing here on a Saturday?"

"Duh. He *has* to be here. It's graduation day."

Chapter Nine

Shelly

The two of them sit quietly in Michael's car.

Shelly feels an emptiness envelop her. In a few hours they will be released into the world. She glances at Michael, sure of two things: he needs to meet his father, and he will be better off when she leaves for college. He just doesn't know it yet.

She takes one of Michael's hands in hers. "I remember the first time I saw you sleeping out here."

He grins. "And that's when you knew you had met the man of your dreams?"

"Ha ha. More like my nightmares."

"You chose me, remember?"

She did choose him, and she wonders why. Sure, he's good-looking in a ragged way, like a cowboy who's fallen off his horse and lost his hat. But it was more than that. Something sparked inside when he looked at her, and she recognized another lost soul from her home planet. Can two damaged souls complete one another, or will they create bigger holes?

"Let's go see if the ducks are still here," she says. Shelly and Michael stroll toward the back fence. Shelly spots the birds in the center of the pond. "There they are!"

"They brought friends," Michael says.

Shelly leans against him "Should we have one last kiss by the back fence?"

Michael gazes at her. "Are you saying this is the last time you ever plan to kiss me?"

She knows he's kidding, but Shelly knows this could, in fact, be one of their last kisses. She has to look away. "Don't be maudlin, Neruda," she whispers.

"If you want me to shut up, you have to kiss me."

Shelly knots her arms around his neck and pulls him toward her. She closes her eyes. Through his lips she tastes his past–a boy frolicking barefoot in a park, chasing his brother–and she feels his future—Michael driving a different car, a sedan this time. It has a dented rear bumper and one of the car's wheels is missing a hubcap. The back seat is littered with used books and junk food wrappers.

Both of these images take place in Rooster, Ohio.

But Shelly also imagines an alternate future, one where Michael strides across a college campus of old red brick buildings mixed with modern glass and concrete structures.

Shelly is startled, but not surprised, that she's absent from both scenarios. The end of their story is speeding toward them like a train. She knows it's coming, but that doesn't make it hurt less.

She shakes those thoughts away and nods toward the high school. "Should we go inside?"

"Aren't you afraid Earl and Hess will put us to work?"

Shelly links her arm in his and they stride to the service entrance. "That's the chance we'll have to take."

As soon as they step inside the building Shelly hears Earl's gravelly voice, followed by laughter. Shelly pokes her head in the door of the staff lounge. Hess, Earl and two other custodians are sitting at a round table, drinking coffee. "You call this working?" she says.

"Been waiting for you two," Earl barks.

Chapter Ten

May 28
Shelly

Two days after graduation Shelly glances out her bedroom window at Josh, lying by the pool reading. She always envied kids like her brother who knew exactly what they wanted to do when they headed to college. She barely knows what she's going to do in the next hour, much less the next four years.

She changes into a bikini and goes down to join Josh. She flicks her towel at him before she sits in a lounge chair. He gives her the finger.

"Why are you reading a textbook?" Shelly asks. "It's summer."

"I'm taking an online summer class."

Shelly glances at the title of the book. *Fundamentals of Global Economics.* "Sounds like perfect beach reading."

Josh sets his book down. "Hey, who was that pretty dark-haired girl Michael spent a lot of time talking to at your party?"

"His jailbait sixteen-year-old sister."

"Too bad." Josh stands, flexes his arms and slaps his washboard abs. "She'll miss out on all this."

Shelly laughs, and Josh dives into the pool. Shelly takes off her sunglasses and joins her brother in the water. He splashes her and she tries to dunk him.

They bob in the pool like buoys. "How old were you when you knew you wanted to major in economics?" she asks.

He considers this. "Twelve or so, I guess."

"Why?"

Josh arches an eyebrow. "*Why*? We all have to become something."

"But what made you think, 'Oh man, I can't be a lowly rock star or a famous ball player; I need to become an economist!'"

He chuckles and splashes her. "I've always liked math and history."

"I've never felt a burning need to do anything other than read books and smoke cigarettes."

"One can't major in smoking."

She splashes him back. "I know that, dipshit."

"Major in English. I understand that's good preparation for becoming a barista."

"Shut up!" She swishes water at his face.

"There will always be a need for coffee makers and bartenders. Trust me. I'm an economics major."

She floats on her back. "I can't major in English. That's what Michael's majoring in."

"So?"

"He'll think I'm copying him."

"Since when do you care what anyone thinks?"

Shelly arcs her arms and backstrokes across the pool. Normally she doesn't care, but lately things between her and Michael seesaw between love and animosity. His initial reaction to her getting him into the writing program shocked her. She's glad he calmed down and realized this *is* the best thing for him.

But did she really think Michael would be okay with her going to school in Maryland? Michael has to know they have no future.

Josh swims up next to her. "Most of my friends at school didn't have much of an idea their first couple of semesters, either. But once you start taking courses, you get an idea of what you're good at and also what you enjoy."

"You think?"

"My roommate switches his major every week. One week he wants to be an anthropologist, and the next he swears he's majoring in French literature."

"Really?"

"It all depends on what girl he's dating and whether or not he failed a test."

Shelly dog paddles in circles. "When I ran off with Theo, I wanted to study the Beat writers like he did."

"You still can."

"I just don't want to be one of those girls who do a thing because that's what her boyfriend does."

"Part of why you like those guys is shared interest, so why wouldn't you pursue something similar?"

Shelly gazes at her brother. "I never thought of it that way." She draws back her arm and drenches him with a wave of water. "You're not totally worthless."

He splashes back. "But *you* are!"

Shelly squeals, and the two of them saturate the concrete from another water battle. Eventually, they lie down on the lounge chairs. Shelly wraps herself in her beach towel. "When you left for college, how did you end things with Megan?"

"Why? Are you planning to break up with Michael?"

"I'm going to be in Maryland the next four years, and I don't see myself coming back here once I get my degree."

Josh nods. "Yeah, I get that. Megan was born and raised here. Her whole family lives here. I couldn't picture a future for us, either."

Shelly crosses her arms. "Why did Mom and Dad even bring us here?"

"They thought they were keeping us out of trouble."

"Yeah, that worked out well."

He laughs. "You could live alone on a desert island and still manage to fall into deep shit."

Shelly smirks, knowing this is true. "How do I break it off without hurting him?"

"Good luck with that." Josh scuffs his wet hair with his towel. "If he cares about you as much as he appears to, breaking up will sucker punch him."

Shelly rolls to face her brother. "I'm hoping once he meets his father he'll stay in Seattle. That way the problem solves itself."

Josh stretches out on his chair. "There's a chance he won't. Didn't you say he hasn't even contacted the guy?"

"Yes. And I don't understand why. He's wanted to meet him his whole life."

Josh rests his head on his arm. "When I found out you're really my cousin instead of my sister, it threw me for a loop. And that's minor compared to meeting your father for the first time."

"It will be the best thing for him."

"Did you really fill out his application and engineer his scholarship?"

She nods.

"You should go into business management," Josh says.

"That's what Michael said! But I want something glamorous."

"You're pushy as hell. Why not use that to be a Hollywood agent?"

"Do I need a degree to do that?"

"It would help provide business credentials."

"So, do I *have* to major in business?"

"Not necessarily. A degree shows you can commit to something. Major in English and become a literary agent."

"And when Michael writes his novel, I'll make him rich and famous."

Josh studies her. "Are you sure you want to dump him? You two care about each other."

"It's…. best for both of us."

"How do you know?" Josh asks.

"The other day, when I went with him to his brother's graduation party, I felt like I was in a foreign country. There were junky cars parked on the lawn, and the house was so messy and small. I don't want to sound all judgy, but that's not the future I want."

"And you think if you stay with him you'll end up in poverty."

"It's not just that." Shelly wraps her arms around herself. "You've met me. I'm a horrible person. Totally unreliable. I'm like that awful Gretchen in *You're the Worst*."

Josh laughs. "You *are* her."

"But Michael isn't like the awful Jimmy. He deserves better. I mean, he has an edge, and a bad temper, but underneath it all, he's a nice guy."

Josh flops onto his stomach. "Whatever you do, try not to burn all your bridges."

"Do you and Megan still talk?"

"Occasionally."

"Friends with benefits?"

"Nah. She's seeing someone else."

"Sorry."

He sighs. "I'll always care about her, but we're totally wrong for each other."

"Sounds like me and Michael." Shelly reaches over and taps her brother's hand. "Thanks for listening."

"Just doing my job as your big brother."

Chapter Eleven
June 2
Michael

Shelly's number pops up while I'm in the middle of a run. Normally I wouldn't answer, but it may be about the trip. I slow down and say, "I'm sexy and I know it."

Her voice is garbled. "Michael…"

I come to a stop. "Are you okay?"

"My…my father found out what happened to my birth mother," she says. "He hired someone to find her, and … he came back with a copy of her death certificate."

"I'll be right over."

***

Shelly is slumped in a lawn chair next to the pool when I get there, her face resting on her fist.

"Hey," I say, and lie on the lounge chair next to her. She lets me wrap her in my arms as she weeps. "I'm so sorry, Shel." I don't know what else to say, so I just let her cry until she feels like talking.

"Why does this bug me so much?" she asks. "It's not like I'm surprised. I knew she was an addict."

"What happened to her?"

Shelly pulls a new tissue out of the box and dabs her face. "She died of pneumonia about two years after she reached San Francisco. My dad couldn't find out many details, but she was homeless."

She begins to cry again. "From what my mom told me, my mother had a sucky, sucky life her last few years, and now I find out she had a sucky, sucky death."

Shelly blows her nose. "I don't remember her at all, and now I'll never have that chance."

After Shelly's tears run dry, we sit by the pool and dangle our feet in the water. "I envy you, Neruda."

"Why?"

"You know your mother."

"Ha! She's not even speaking to me."

"But you know her, and you also know she loves you."

At graduation my mom had stood at the edge of the bleachers next to Earl. She wore her work uniform, and stayed long enough to watch Jeff and me receive our diplomas, but I couldn't find her afterwards.

"And now you have a chance to meet your dad," Shelly adds. "You get to put the pieces of your life together and not have huge holes." She splashes her feet in the water and rests her head on my shoulder. "I have a great family, but they only fill part of the gap inside me. I'll never know *either* of the people who created me, so I'll never fully understand why I am the way I am." She wipes her face with her hand. "Everything about me is a myth."

She reaches for a Marlboro and lights it. "Did I ever tell you about how I started smoking?"

I chuff a laugh. "You said you were born holding a lit cigarette."

She takes a puff. "My mother was addicted to nicotine among other things." She expels smoke. "The first time cigarettes drew me was when I was ten. We still lived in Cleveland, and my dad's law firm sponsored a day on the lake. There were kids of all ages. Josh tried his best to ditch me late in the afternoon when he and three of the other boys wandered off. But torturing my brother has always been a high point of my life." She grins at me.

"Nice to know I'm not the only one you torment," I say.

She looks down at the pool and swirls her feet in the blue water. "Anyway, I followed them because I had a crush on a fourteen-year-old named Lachlan Speer. He looked like Harry Styles.

"The boys and I trudged to a part of the beach out of sight of parental units. It was hot, and none of us thought to bring anything to drink. Lachlan handed one of the boys a ten-dollar bill and told him to buy us all Cokes. The other kid went with him, so it was just Lachlan, Josh, and me. We sat in a circle and Lachlan pulled a mangled pack of *Winstons* out of his shorts. He'd noticed me admiring his smoke rings, and said, "Want to learn how? I'll teach you."

"Sure," I replied.

Holding his own cigarette, Josh said, "Shelly, Mom will kill you for smoking,".

"Don't be a buzz kill, man," Lachlan said.

"But she's only ten."

I extracted a cigarette and placed it between my lips. Lachlan leaned over and flicked his lighter. Josh looked away and dug his feet in the sand. Lachlan told me to inhale, then let it go.

"At first the tobacco was horrible, and I wondered why people smoked. Yet with the second puff, the slow burn felt like a warm hand on my forehead on a chilly night.

"By the time the two other boys came back with their drinks, I was blowing smoke rings like a pro."

Shelly takes a long inhale. "After that day I craved the feel and taste of cigarettes."

***

As I drive home, I think of how Shelly and I are bound by absence. Her father died before she was born, and she was abandoned by her birth mother. I've never known my father, and my mother is half there at best.

Sure, my mom is bat-shit crazy, but she's alive and only a few miles away.

I glance at my gas gauge. The Blue Whale has a quarter of a tank. It's enough to make it to Mom's and then back to Earl's farm.

The last time I saw my mother, I drove Annie over to pick up some of her clothes. Mom marched across her lawn and exploded at me with every expletive imaginable. She pounded on my chest with her fists. "Thanks to you, social services are all up my ass!"

"Mom, you need help."

She stood spitting distance from my face. "None of this would have happened if Earl hadn't found out you lived in your damn car!"

"I wouldn't have lived in The Whale in the first place if this house was habitable," I yelled back.

I park The Whale in front of Mom's car. The smell of cigarette smoke emanates from an open second floor window. I knock on the front door.

"What do you want?"

I look up. My mother is leaning out of her bedroom window.

"Hi, Mom."

"Get the hell off my property."

"I just wanted to…"

She disappears, then reappears and throws something down at me. It bounces off my shoulder. "I said go away you ungrateful little shit."

I pick up the old sandal she threw at me. "You're not getting this back! May as well toss the other one!"

She hurls a clock and a stack of magazines. It occurs to me if I stand here long enough she'll toss out a whole roomful of junk. But suddenly, she slams the window shut.

I cup my hands around my mouth and shout, "just wanted to let you know I'm going to Seattle!" I gather up the discarded items and add, "I love you!"

I carry the junk she tossed to the dumpster. Throwing away my mother's castoffs doesn't bring me the satisfaction I expected.

Chapter Twelve
June 5
Michael

Shelly insists I take the window seat since this is my first flight. "I feel like I swallowed broken glass, and not just because we might bite the dust at thirty thousand feet in the air."

"Statistically, flying is the safest way to die," she says, and grins at me.

"What?"

She bumps her shoulder into mine and bats her baby blues. "I'm teasing, silly."

"I hate you so much."

I turn my face toward the window and watch guys in neon yellow vests load bags onto the plane. The muffled chatter, the click of seat belts, the slam bang of bags stowed overhead, a crying baby, and the stench of jet fuel wafting in from the open door are all too much. Bile rises in my throat. I unhook my seat belt and try to stand. "I've changed my mind. This whole thing is a terrible idea."

Shelly pulls on my arm. "Calm down, Neruda. We'll be fine."

"It's not just the flight."

"Michael." She narrows her eyes. "Isn't this what you've wanted your whole life?"

The future is an empty distance. The present is no prize, either, but it's what I know. "I need more time to prepare."

"You've had almost a year."

I groan and bang my head against the headrest.

"Look." She points out the window. "It's a beautiful day. Nothing horrible is going to happen."

"Ha! My mother used to say bad things didn't happen on sunny days, and we both know what a reliable source she is."

A flight attendant walks up and down the aisle, closing overhead bins and eyeing passengers. She reminds us to fasten our seat belts. The front door slams and the plane wobbles. I click my seatbelt in place. "I guess there's no turning back now."

At the end of the runway the engines roar, the plane shimmies, and suddenly we're jettisoned into the air as if tossed by a giant's hand. The plane ascends at a steady rate, and soon the pilot announces we're at thirty thousand feet.

"The worst part is over, you know," Shelly says. "That is until we land."

"What do you mean?"

"Landings are the second most dangerous part of a flight."

I glare at her. "You're such a comforting travel companion."

"Yeah, but you can't survive without me." She wraps her hands around my arm and snuggles against my shoulder.

"I'll be on my own once you abandon me for Baltimore."

She sighs and plops back in her seat. "Can we save that argument for another time?"

"We always do."

She tosses me her *People,* covers herself with her jean jacket, and rests against my shoulder. "I need to get some sleep."

"How long is this flight?"

"Five hours to L.A. Then another two to Seattle."

I give her a devilish grin. "Can you go that long without a cigarette?"

She buries her head under her jacket. "Ugh. Thanks for reminding me. Now we're both doomed."

The plane dips and shudders and I grip the hand rest. Below us the landscape is an unlined map.

Shelly pokes her head from under her jacket. "Everything will be okay, Neruda."

"Keep telling me that."

As Shelly tries to sleep, I study her oval face and stroke the long strands of dyed black hair. She knows my worst secrets and she's still with me. Her own mysteries are locked in an underground vault with a missing key.

She burrows deeper against me. I brush the hair away from her face and kiss her forehead. We've seen each other almost every day for a year. Three weeks apart will feel like eternity.

Chapter Thirteen
Michael

A massive thump from below jolts me awake, as if the giant who tossed us in the air now kicks the bottom of the aircraft. "What the hell was that?" I ask.

Shelly yawns and stretches. "Landing gear. You *want* to hear that sound."

The plane wavers and whines as it descends. After a sudden *thwap* onto the tarmac, the jet shrieks down the runway until it comes to a sudden stop. I let out my breath. "That part was cool. I think I like landing."

We have a two-hour layover in Los Angeles and Shelly rushes to the exit so she can take a smoke break.

As we step outside, I say, "we'll have to go through security again,"

She lights her Marlboro, inhales, and then exhales a smokestack-sized plume. "I don't care. This is worth it."

I roll my eyes and set my backpack at my feet. "You'll be happy to know I finally emailed my father this morning."

She takes another long drag from her cigarette. "What did you say to him?"

"I took your suggestion and wrote it as a story."

Her eyebrows shoot up. "Read it to me."

I pull out the laptop Earl and Dot gave me for graduation and open the message.

Dear Dr. Meadows,
Here is a short story for you:

A tall blonde seventeen-year-old, beautiful in that ragged way of girls who live in trailers, sits down next to her crush. He doesn't reciprocate the infatuation, not initially anyway. He's only here to tutor her in science for service learning credit. She's not the kind of girl a guy like him- popular, athletic, and rich- would mix with.

Except soon, he grows to like the girl. She's funny without trying, cute in her candor and self-deprecation. But they aren't friends, at least not publicly.

He has a steady- a cliquish cheerleader who is like one of the Mean Girls, but he's been dating her so long he doesn't really know how to get rid of her. It's a small town and the pickings are slim.

And this blonde girl dates some guy who drives a jacked-up car with a loud muffler. So, he and the girl aren't really friends or lovers.

Yet there's something about her. She makes him laugh, and after the science lessons he feels better about life for a while. He wishes he could spend more time with her.

Then, at Homecoming they have a nice moment outside after both of them had arguments with their dates. They enjoy a joint and some French kissing together against the side of the building. Yet still, he has his set of friends, his irascible girlfriend, and his winning athletic ability. Besides, what does he have in common with this blonde?

In the course of their lessons, though, which have evolved more into conversations about life and the future and less about science, the boy discovers that he and his protégée share the same lunch period, and he coaxes her into meeting him privately a couple times a week. He knows of a place, he tells her, where the world can be all their own, their own secret hideaway.

The girl, named Susan, meanwhile, breaks up with her redneck boyfriend. She doesn't want a future in this town, and loud-muffler-boy-with-the-mullet-haircut has no intention of leaving. She wants someone like this boy, the good-looking science tutor, whose future is mapped out a long way from Rooster, Ohio.

Yet in a confluence of tragedies, Susan's brother dies on graduation day, and shortly afterwards the boy's father drives his Alfa Romeo into a lake, and their story ends. Except it doesn't, because the boy and girl have mixed their DNA, and eighteen years later their son finally learns who his father is.

My name is Michael Flynn, and I will be participating in the Hugo House Summer of Writing program in Seattle between June 7-June 28 if you care to meet me.

I close the computer and slide it back in my bag. "I included my phone number."

Shelly takes a final drag and smashes the butt in a nearby ash can. She walks away, appearing to contemplate. She pulls another cigarette out of her bag. "You used my phrase, 'confluence of tragedies.'"

"I'll be sure to mention you in my Pulitzer acceptance speech."

Shelly lights her second cigarette, inhales as if she's facing a firing squad, and slowly expels her smoke. "I'm glad you didn't send him one of those poems where you wanted to kill him. He's less likely to call the SWAT Team."

"Ha ha. So, what do you think?"

"I think you nailed it."

"Yeah?"

She takes a giant puff and exhales. "It's perfect."

"I think by taking his point of view it kind of helped me understand how confused he felt about my mother. And who knows? If my uncle Gil and his father hadn't died, I may have grown up tagging sea turtles."

Shelly stumps out the rest of her second cig and slings her bag over her shoulder. "Now that he knows about you, what will you do?"

I pick up my own bag and we saunter inside the airport. "Avoid checking my email and phone for the rest of my life."

She scowls at me. "Why? What are you so afraid of?"

Two films stream inside my head: one where Dr. Ashton Meadows welcomes me into his life and we all live happily ever after. The other reel shows my father shouting at me to get the hell out of his life and never contact him again or he will sue my white-trash ass.

"Everything."

We move up a few spaces in the security line and she wraps her arms around my waist. "This whole trip is such an adventure for you. You're like Lawrence of Arabia without a camel."

I stifle a laugh, fully aware that uniformed guards scan our every move. Shelly may not mind spending time in jail again, but I sure as hell don't want to go back there.

I hand the security dude my real driver's license, not the one where I'm twenty-two-year-old Michael F. Neruda.

After going through security, we have just enough time to use the bathroom, find the gate, and board the flight to Seattle, where I get to experience the terror of takeoff and the thrill of landing all over again.

***

Shelly's never been to Seattle, yet she weaves through the terminal as if she works here. We reach Baggage Claim and suddenly she leaps into some guy's arms and plants a big kiss on his lips.

Shelly never mentioned what Theo looked like. When I imagined her ex, a grad student in Literature, I pictured a skinny guy with pale skin and stringy hair, not some younger version of Rob Lowe.

Not that I'm an ogre. Shelly wouldn't date me if I weren't passably handsome, but next to Theo, I resemble something from the bottom of a laundry basket.

Why did I agree that we should stay with her ex? Oh yeah, because Shelly makes all our decisions.

Theo's eyes walk all over her. "Valentine, you look spectacular."

Valentine? Then it hits me; when they were together in California, Shelly went by her birth name, Valentine Falls.

"So do you!" She gazes up at Theo. I clear my throat to remind her I'm standing here.

"Theo, this is Michael. Michael, Theo."

My fingers wave caution flags as Theo firmly grips my hand, and I notice his arm has the chiseled quality of someone well acquainted with weight training. Shelly had said Theo was twenty-four, so he's allegedly only five years older than me, but the lines around his eyes tell a different story.

"You guys ready to hit the town?" he asks.

Shelly and I follow him as we wheel our suitcases toward the exit. "We're taking the light rail downtown, and I thought we'd stop near Pike Place Market and get something to eat and maybe wander around before I take you to my castle."

Theo's so handsome and charming he probably *does* live in a castle. I hate this guy.

Not sure what a light rail is, but I'm guessing it's a train of some sort.

We trek for almost a mile through a covered concrete walkway toward the tracks, yet the walk feels good after being pretzled into an airplane seat. Theo helps us buy tickets and we stand on a platform to wait for the transport. I want to tell Shelly this is also my first train ride, but I don't want to look like a toothless hick in front of her ex.

The train screeches to a stop, the doors slide open, and the three of us board. Shelly scoots next to Theo, and I'm stuck across the aisle next to a guy wearing a red turban and brown pajamas.

The rail car lurches forward and quickly gains speed. I gaze at the map posted on the ceiling and notice we have a dozen stops before the University of Washington.

The train travels over a highway where traffic seems at a standstill. We pass miles and miles of cargo trailers, high rise apartments, rickety houses, office buildings, strip malls, and railroad tracks. In Rooster, most people are surrounded by open fields and massive yards. Here, it looks as if people live and work stacked on top of one another.

Theo and Shelly start talking. I lean away from the turban headed dude to be included in their conversation and hear Shelly say, "Remember what you guys did to me in the desert?"

Theo chuckles. "You were so..."

"You went to the desert?" I interject. They both look at me oddly, so I make it worse. "I mean, I didn't think there were any deserts in San Francisco."

"It was in Arizona," Theo says. "On our way out to California."

"Oh, sure." I nod, and retreat back to my seat. Clearly, I'm the third wheel.

The train slows and an electronic voice calls out, "Next stop, Rainier Beach." Near the tracks I spot a sign for a Polynesian Deli. I'm definitely not in Rooster, Ohio anymore.

After a few stops, the loudspeaker announces, "Next stop Westlake Station." Theo stands. "We'll get off here first."

The three of us hustle off the train. Theo taps what looks like a credit card against a yellow machine and we ascend an escalator to the street exit. I squint in the sun. "I thought it rained here all the time."

"Summers in Seattle are pleasant and warm," he says.

"Not like San Francisco," Shelly says, and shivers.

Her mentioning their shared past reminds me she'll be spending two nights alone with Theo after I move into the dorm.

I give Theo the stink eye, but he isn't even looking at me.

Theo leads us a couple of blocks to a nearby coffee shop where we order drinks and pastries, and cram ourselves around a tiny table. I hold my croissant in my lap rather than trying to fit it on the shoebox sized table.

Theo reaches for his cup, and I'm reminded how his biceps look like they're sculpted from marble. I hate this guy's fearless, strong body, and hate that Shelly knows how that body feels next to hers.

Shelly's ex takes a bite from his chocolate croissant, and asks, "What do you guys want to do while you're here?"

"Michael wants to explore some bookstores," Shelly says.

So, she does know I'm here.

"We have tons of them." He wipes his mouth with a pocket-sized napkin. "Left Bank Books is just up the street. We'll go there next."

My feelings toward Theo thaw slightly, but I still want to kick his ass.

"How's the dissertation coming?" Shelly asks.

"Nearly finished." He sips his espresso. "I have to rewrite three chapters, and resubmit."

Shelly claps her hands. "Then you'll be Dr. Garibaldi."

"Yep. I fly back to Columbus to defend in August."

"Do you have a job lined up?" she asks.

"Not at a university, but I've been doing writing workshops at Hugo House." He looks at me. "In fact, I'm one of the instructors at the summer workshop."

"Small world," I say.

Theo raises his cup. "Indeed."

Just as I'm about to take a bite of my pastry, he says, "I hear you lived in your car for a while."

I spear Shelly with a look.

"I figured it's no big secret now," she says.

"But it's *my* secret, and I don't feel like sharing it with the world."

Shelly gives me a fake apologetic look. I gnaw on my pastry.

"Have you written about it?" Theo asks.

"No. Mostly, I'd like to forget the whole experience."

"As Hemingway would say, you're strong at the broken places," Theo says. "Make your journey to the *now* a thing of beauty. That's why we read stories. Not to hear how great someone's life is, but how they persevered through misery and despair."

I look at Shelly so we can roll our eyes together, but instead of mocking Theo's pretensions, she's gazing at him like a devoted fan.

"You must be a good writer to have gotten into this program. It's highly competitive." Theo says to me.

"Thanks."

We finish our coffee and walk a short way up a tourist filled street. "You can't come to Seattle and not see Pike Place Market," Theo says.

He guides us inside a slim bookshop where each wall is covered floor to ceiling with books.

"It's kind of hit or miss here," Theo says. "You wait for a book to call you rather than try to find something specific."

"Sounds like the Cemetery of Forgotten Books," I say.

Theo nods. "*Shadow of the Wind*. Great book."

"That's Michael's favorite book!" Shelly says.

I lean in and whisper, "Did you tell him that ahead of time to get me to like him?"

"Seriously, Neruda?"

We separate to browse. A thin paperback called *Too Loud a Solitude* by Bohumil Hrabal calls to me. It's about a man who works as a paper shredder, but he keeps some of the books he is supposed to shred. According to the cover it was banned in Europe.

The woman at the cash register glances at the cover. "Great book."

I thank her and stash the paperback in the side pocket of my suitcase.

Shelly and I follow Theo up the street to the entrance of a giant open market where guys are throwing raw fish at one another. A crowd gathers to watch, but the fish smell nauseates Shelly.

Theo takes us inside a spice store where our luggage crowds the aisles. He buys some tea and cardamom and we amble by several more shops. The crowds are unsettling, and I'm relieved when Theo says, "Let's get out of here."

Back outside, he says, "Let's hit the underground grocery store."

A few blocks later Theo leads us onto an escalator going down.

"It really *is* underground," I say.

Theo eyes me. "What did you think I meant?"

"A secret passageway or a shadowy looking guy guarding the door?"

Theo laughs, and we go down the escalator. Shelly chooses two bottles of wine. "The first time I bought wine with Michael he thought Boone's Farm was real wine."

I flare my nostrils at her. "You just love making me look bad, don't you?"

"No. I think it's funny is all."

Theo pats me on the back. "I think Boone's Farm was the first wine I drank, too."

We trek back to Westlake Station and catch the light rail to the University District. I practically vault into a seat next to Shelly, forcing Theo to stand and hold a handrail.

At Theo's stop we follow him and wheel our bags for a couple of blocks, uphill, to a white house with a ragged lawn. "Home sweet home," Theo says.

He unlocks a door and we haul our stuff up a flight of stairs. "We'll need to be quiet because my roommate, Dale, sleeps in the daytime."

He opens door B, and a well-fed orange cat jumps off the arm of a chair. Theo scratches and pets its head. "This is Yab Yum," he whispers. "He adopted us after our neighbor in A moved out and left him behind."

The living room walls are stacked high with books, and there's only enough space for two chairs, a coffee table, the bookcases, and a couple of lamps. "This apartment isn't much bigger than The Blue Whale," I whisper to Shelly.

Each of us takes turns using the toilet. While Theo is in the bathroom, I snoop through Theo's large collection of CDs and vinyl. Miles Davis, John Coltrane, Gil Scott-Heron, Luther Allison. "Damn. It's bad enough he's handsome and intelligent, but he's got good taste in music, too. What *do* you see in me?"

"You're damaged," Shelly says. "I like that in a guy."

Theo's apartment has two-bedrooms, but since he has a roommate, Theo offers Shelly and me his room. "I'll take one of the recliners," he says. "I often end up sleeping in one of them anyway."

We stash our bags in his room, and Theo asks, "Do you guys want to rest or sightsee?" Theo asks.

"Sightsee," Shelly and I say in unison.

The three of us step outside and head for a bus stop. "You'll love Gas Works Park," Theo says. "It has a great view of Lake Union and Seattle."

At the bus stop my phone buzzes. Shelly gives me a hopeful look. "Your father?"

I pull out my phone. "Paul." I read the message. "What the hell?"

"What's the matter, Neruda?"

"Paul says my mom tripped on her steps and broke her arm."

Theo and Shelly exchange a glance. I stash my phone back in my pocket. "I knew something like this would happen. I should go home."

"Michael, I've seen her living room. She would have broken her arm whether or not you left."

I gnaw on my cuticle. Shelly adds, "Besides, she's a grown-up."

"Barely."

The bus pulls up and Shelly pushes me toward it. "You're staying."

At our stop, Theo says, "It's a bit of a hike, but it's worth the effort." We trudge uphill about half a mile, when suddenly, monstrous smokestacks loom at the crest.

"Whoa. It's like we reached the end of the world," I say.

"It's so Mad Max," Shelly says.

"This was once a working oil refinery," Theo says. "Now it's just a great place to chill."

On a nearby slope a group of kids slide down a home-made water slide. "Jeff and I used to do that when we were kids," I say. "There was a small grassy hill near the dumpsters of our apartment complex and we created a water slide out of a shower curtain we found in the trash."

"Ew. Didn't it have mold on it?" Shelly asks.

"We set the moldy side down. Eventually it wore off."

The three of us step down to a platform overlooking the lake. A low-flying plane passes above. I look up and feel a wave of dizziness. I grip the rail.

Shelly touches my arm. "You look exhausted, Neruda. Maybe we should go back to Theo's and take a nap."

"Yeah, you guys should probably rest," Theo says.

I puff my chest out. "I'm fine. I may even climb one of these smokestacks."

"Uh, I think you'd get arrested, Neruda."

"Whatever."

Theo pulls away to answer a phone call. Shelly grabs my hand and leads me to a grassy spot overlooking the lake. She pushes me down and collapses next to me. "Why are you trying to pretend you're not tired?"

I shoot a glance at Theo.

"Really, Neruda? You're trying to impress Theo?"

"I just don't want him to see me as weak and lazy."

She shoves me. "Get over yourself and take a nap."

I roll on my side and reach for her. "Guess what, Dorothy? We're not in Kansas anymore."

She snickers, "No, Toto, we are not." We snuggle in the sun and she links her fingers with mine. "Your mother will be fine."

"In my head I know that. That doesn't mean I'll stop worrying."

"You're too far away to do anything about it now."

I sigh. "Somewhere far away my mother cradles her broken limb, and somewhere near here, my father may or may not have read my note."

Chapter Fourteen
Michael

The short nap at Gas Works Park helps me feel almost alive, and Shelly and I follow Theo back to his apartment.

Theo's roommate Dale is awake. He's a lean guy with a beard and hair halfway down his back. Shelly gives him a hug, and I remember she also knows Dale from her San Francisco days.

After some light-hearted banter, Dale mentions he and Theo are out of bread and coffee.

We pile into Dale's car, a 1999 Ford Escort station wagon that reminds me of The Whale. Dale's car is newer and smaller, but as I run my hand across the tattered back seat, I feel a twinge of nostalgia.

On the way to Trader Joe's, Dale says, "You know, when you've seen one shopping center, you've seen the mall."

I laugh, and Theo and Shelly both let out groans. "Don't encourage him," Theo says, "or he'll never stop."

"Two peanuts walk into a bar," Dale says. "One was a salted."

I can't help but laugh again

"See what I mean? Dale has a new audience, so he's breaking you in."

As Dale drives, he pumps out a couple more. "The Invisible Man marries the Invisible Woman. The kids were nothing to look at, though. A couple of cannibals start eating a clown. One looks at the other and asks, 'does this taste funny to you?'" Dale wiggles his eyebrows. He adds. "I'm reading a book about anti-gravity. It's impossible to put down. "Is it me, or are circles just pointless?"

I'm starting to see what Theo means.

In the vegetable aisle, Dale strokes his beard and holds up an ear of corn. "You know, thieves who steal ears of corn commit acts of stalking."

"Enough!" Theo barks. Dale feigns a frown and sets the corn back in the bin.

In the dairy case, Shelly hands Dale an egg. "Okay Dale, do your magic. Last one for the night." She whispers to me. "This one is classic."

Dale grins, strikes a regal pose, and holds up the egg. "A hardboiled egg sure is hard to beat."

I give Dale a wicked grin. "Yes, but a chicken crossing the road is poultry in motion."

Dale smiles and bows. Shelly rolls her eyes. "Oh God, Theo, now there's two of them."

I spring for a couple of frozen pizzas, and Theo and Dale buy a twelve pack of Olympia beer. Theo picks up a case of red wine. "This is a good blend for the price, and I know our girl here likes red."

His use of *our girl* makes me cringe.

On the drive back to the apartment, I miss the puns. It's as if Dale powered down.

As we eat, Theo says, "Did Val mention we met on my Kerouac page?"

Theo calling Shelly Val pokes at me like a porcupine spine; it's a constant reminder of their shared past. "She told me the whole San Francisco saga. Bed bugs and all."

"Do you still have the page?" Shelly asks.

"It's still up," Theo says, "but it's been awhile since I've updated it."

"Do you still have bed bugs?" I ask.

"Michael!" Shelly says.

"Just kidding." Well, sort of.

"I assure you, Dale and I are bed bug free," Theo says.

After dinner, Dale drives us to a poetry reading at Elliot Bay Books. The store is jam-packed with people. "There won't be enough seats for the four of us."

"I'll just stand," I say.

"Me, too, "Shelly says. "We've been sitting all day."

The store manager says a few opening remarks, and introduces the poet, Billy Collins.

"He doesn't look like a poet," I whisper to Shelly. "He looks like our high school principal."

"Not all poets dress like ironic hipsters," she whispers back.

"I'd like to begin with an early poem," Collins says. He glances down at the page. "It's called 'Writing in the Afterlife.'"

I'm enjoying the reading until Collins comes to a poem he calls, "The Lanyard." The speaker in this poem is a boy who proudly gives his mother a lanyard he makes at summer camp, imagining it's enough of a payback for her raising and nurturing him. As Collins finishes, a tightness grips my chest.

What have I done to my own mother? My payback for raising me was inviting Social Services to her home. And now I'm here for the ultimate betrayal: to meet the man she never wanted me to know.

"I'll be right back," I tell Shelly.

The throngs of people inside this store fuel my anxiety, and it's hard to breathe. I shove past them up the stairs to the exit.

Near the store's entrance I notice a guy a few yards away, smoking. He's long-haired and bearded, but too clean to be a vagrant. This is one of the times I wish I smoked. I get it now; smoking gives you something to do with your hands, something to take your mind off yourself and your foul deeds.

Sure, my childhood was wonky, but Mom loved us. I repaid her by inviting social workers into her bottomless pit.

My mother works as a nurse's aide in an assisted living facility, so she has access to people who can help her, but her co-workers and patients probably don't know she needs help. Mom appears normal. She shows up to work on time, assists her patients and works well with the staff. They return the love by giving her things.

She knows she has a problem, but to her the hordes of rubbish are 'something she'll get to eventually.' But eventually never comes. And now all that shit is trying to kill her.

I lean against the building, slide to my haunches, and check my phone. No texts or calls from a 206 prefix. I don't deserve a relationship with my father anyway. I have nothing to add to his life. What the hell am I doing here?

"I shouldn't have sent him that email," I mutter.

"Hey, buddy, are you okay?" The smoker appears in front of me.

"Yeah, thanks." I stand and stash my phone in my side pocket. "Just a little jet lag."

He nods. "Want a hit?" He's not smoking a cigarette.

"Sure." The dude hands me the joint, and I take a toke. It's been awhile, so I cough and pass it back to him.

"Where are you from?" the guy asks.

"Ohio. Just flew in today."

"That's a long way." He hands me the bud again and I take a second hit. "Another time zone."

I nod. "It's like midnight my time." The joint is almost gone, so I give it back to the dude. "Don't you worry you'll get arrested for smoking weed?"

"Pot's legal in Washington."

"Good to know."

"Are you here for the reading?"

"Yeah. It was a little tight in there," I say.

The stranger takes the final hit. "I'm not comfortable in crowds, either."

"Thanks for sharing. I'd better get back inside. My girlfriend will wonder what happened to me."

"Glad I could help a guy out."

We shake hands, and I weave my way back to Shelly and Theo. Shelly sniffs and gives me a shit-eating grin.

"I'd like to end with a new poem," Mr. Collins says. I only half listen because I'm a little stoned.

When Collins finishes, he receives thunderous applause, and the manager announces the poet will now sign books. Shelly pulls me toward the signing table.

"Come on, stoner boy," she says. "I need to get my book signed."

As we wait, she whispers, "Where'd you find pot?"

"I met a guy outside who shared his joint. It's legal here."

Shelly gets her book signed and asks if I want to look around the store.

"I'd kind of like to get something to eat."

We find Theo and Dale. "Michael's stoned and has the munchies," Shelly says.

"We've got food and wine back at our place," Theo says.

"I need to get ready for work anyway," Dale says.

"Where do you work?" I ask.

"I'm a security guard at University Medical Center. The 11-7:30 shift. I take odd jobs for the experience as well as the money."

"Dale's trying to relive Orwell's experiences of being down and out in London, except here in Seattle," Theo says.

"I tried doing that in San Francisco," Shelly says. "Poverty is overrated."

Chapter Fifteen
Michael

Dale heads for the shower and Theo uncorks a bottle of red and pours each of us a glass. I carry a big bowl of popcorn and the three of us cram into the tiny living room and sit on the carpet. "I almost forgot to give you your gift, Theo." Shelly scrambles up and roots around in her luggage.

She brings Theo a DVD of *On the Road*. "I'm sure you've seen this but thought you might want to own a copy."

"Wow. Thank you."

She sits cross legged and grabs a handful of popcorn. "Did you like the movie when you first saw it?"

"It's not the best rendition of the novel, but it opens *On the Road* to a new audience." He places the DVD on the bookshelf.

"The film never made it to Rooster," Shelly says. "We had to drive to Columbus to see it."

"I didn't think the guy who played Kerouac was right for the role," I say.

Shelly spikes me with a look. "Just because you work in a movie theatre doesn't make you an expert on film."

"The rest of the actors were good," I continue. "I loved the Burroughs guy and his freaky wife."

Theo nods. "I think Dean Moriarty was well portrayed, too. That actor captured the combination of bombast and sadness in Dean's character."

Blue Valentines

"Ginsberg and the women were great, also," I add. "Even the vampire girl from *Twilight*."

"You just like her because she showed her titties," Shelly sputters.

"That didn't *hurt* her performance."

Shelly kicks me and I seize one of her bare feet. She wriggles it away, which knocks the bowl and sprinkles kernels of popcorn across the floor. She picks up a handful and pelts me with popcorn.

"I thought the deleted scenes were the best part," I say, needling her.

"My next boyfriend won't even watch movies!" Shelly says.

"The movie *overall* was pretty good," I say, "I just think the Kerouac guy had the wrong energy."

Shelly pokes at my thigh with her free hand. "How do you picture yourself portrayed?

"I don't know. I've never really thought about it. Who do *you* picture playing me?"

She studies me for a few seconds. "An unknown, maybe."

Theo comes back in with another opened bottle of red and fills our wine glasses.

"Who should play Theo?" I ask.

"Chris Hemsworth."

I send her a stinging look. "You've obviously given that a lot of thought."

Shelly jabs me again with her finger. "Okay, movie expert. Who should play Kerouac?"

I gulp some wine and set my glass down. "Someone like James Franco could play him as brooding and sad."

Theo fills his own glass. "Good choice." He plunks into the recliner and sets the bottle next to his feet.

Shelly splays her arms and a few drops of wine trickle down her hand. "But James Franco *always* plays poets."

I gently take her glass and place it on the floor. I'd lick the wine off her fingers, but in her current mood, she might bite me.

"He was in *Howl*," Theo says. "I have it on DVD if you guys want to watch it."

"Sure. Then Shelly can see what I mean about how Franco has the right energy for the role."

She huffs and grabs for her glass. "Fine, if that's what you idiots want."

Dale comes in wearing his quasi cop uniform and stands near the door, his ponytail hidden under his cap. He bids us all good-night.

After Dale shuts the door, Theo pulls the DVD of *Howl* from the shelf and revs up his DVD player. "This film is sort of a documentary. The conceit is it's an interview with Ginsberg, with flashback scenes."

Shelly and I usually cuddle when we watch movies, but I'm sensing an Arctic chill, so I lean against a bookcase. The cat curls into my lap and falls asleep.

In one scene I gesture toward the screen. "See? The Kerouac in *this* movie also has Kerouac's mannerisms down."

"I don't care!" Shelly shouts, which spooks the cat, and it jumps off my lap. "The other guy wasn't that bad."

"Acting is about interpretation," Theo says. "Michael just didn't care for one actor's interpretation of Sal. Keep in mind, Sal Paradise is a fictional depiction."

"But didn't Kerouac base his novel on real relationships?" Shelly asks.

"The focus of *On the Road* is actually Dean Moriarty," Theo says.

"But in the book Sal is at the center. He's the narrator," I say.

"This is a film." Theo says. "It's a different medium."

Shelly bangs her head on the floor and groans. "I'm sick to death of this conversation. Can we just finish the stupid movie?"

The three of us remain silent until the end of the film. Then I say, "I love that line in the court room scene where the one guy says to the lawyer how you can't translate poetry into prose because it's poetry."

"That single line likely won Ferlinghetti's case," Theo says. "The prevailing sentiment at the time was that *Howl* was obscene. All the Beat writers' works were under scrutiny and harsh criticism. Kerouac..."

Shelly clears her throat and glowers at Theo. "Can we talk about anything *but* Kerouac?"

"Sorry," he says. "Ginsberg's writer friend, we'll call him Jim, wrote a lot of books, and he was often bashed by the critics. Ironically, those critics helped Jim sell a lot of books."

"Why is that?" I ask. "How come banned books become bestsellers? Part of what attracted me to the book I bought today was that it was banned."

"It's the paradox of life. We're drawn to what's forbidden."

Over the next several hours the three of us discuss the gamut of topics, including my car and how I managed to live in it, me and Shelly working for Earl and Hess, why she calls me 'Neruda,', the horror of high school, thin crust versus thick crust pizza, vinyl versus CDs, the advantages of legalized marijuana, Theo's dislike of eBooks, Shelly's fear of bats, my disdain for colored paperclips, and finally, why Starbucks is such a big deal.

"Why *are* writers so into coffee shops?" Shelly asks. "Even if the coffee is terrible, they're always full of them."

"We can hang around for hours and not have to spend money," Theo says. "The suits who order the five-dollar lattes subsidize us poor, starving writerly types."

"But they have awful coffee. I can barely *stand* to drink the five-dollar lattes," Shelly says.

"I just add lots of cream," Theo says.

"If you order a *misto*, it's two bucks cheaper than a latte," I say, "and if you add honey and cinnamon, it's almost as good."

"Thanks for the tip."

Shelly growls. "Oh my *God,* can there be two more boring guys on the planet?"

"You've dated both of us," I retort. "What does that say about you?"

"That I have horrible taste in men." Shelly lies on her back, yawns, and points to the window. "Hey look, it's getting light outside."

"What the hell time is it?".

Theo stretches and yawns. "Probably around four-thirty or five. The sun comes up early here in summer."

"We should get some sleep, Neruda. We've been awake for days and drunk way too much wine."

Theo reaches for an Ohio State blanket hanging on the back of one of the chairs. He stretches out on the recliner. "Good night." He turns off the lamp, wraps himself up, and pulls the blanket over his head.

Shelly and I shuffle into Theo's bedroom and fall into bed, which is a mattress on the floor. I spread the comforter over us.

We lie there for a moment, and I ask, "So how come you didn't stick with Theo? He's like an Adonis with a brain."

Shelly nudges against me, the inside spoon, her voice thick with fatigue. "I don't know. Maybe I was too much of a mess back then."

"Oh, and you're so normal now?"

"Shut up."

I glide my fingers along her bare arm and down her body and kiss the back of Shelly's neck.

She jabs me with her elbow and scoots away.

"You know, in the last twenty-four hours I have contacted my unknown father, taken my first flight clear across the country, ridden a train in an enormous city, listened to poetry by a famous poet, smoked a joint with a stranger, and am about to sleep with my girlfriend in her ex-lover's bed. How messed up is my life now?"

Shelly grunts. "Go to sleep, Neruda."

Chapter Sixteen
Michael

The shower's running when I wake, which is unfortunate, because I have to piss like a race horse. Shelly's side of the bed is empty. Maybe she's the one in the shower. I stumble up from the mattress, stretch, and get up to investigate.

Shelly's standing in the kitchen next to the coffee pot. "Morning, sunshine," she says. She's dressed in jeans and a T-shirt. I grunt and pour myself a cup of coffee. She slides a stack of buttered toast toward me on the counter. I pick up a piece and take a bite. The microwave clock says 1:10. "Is that clock right?"

"Yep. We slept all morning."

I sit on the one stool, trying to take my mind off the sound of running water. "I shouldn't have sent that e-mail."

"To your father?"

I nod. "What if his secretary screens his e-mails?"

"You sent it to his work address?"

"It was the only one I could find."

She leans on the counter and thinks for a second. "Well, you didn't come right out and say *he* was your father. If someone else read it, they'd just think you were telling him a story."

The shower stops as I take another bite of toast. "I guess."

"For all anyone knows, you're just some wacked-out student who emailed your professor a short story."

Theo saunters into the kitchen wearing only a towel. He's built like an underwear model, and I hate him all over again.

"I thought I'd take you guys on the ferry to Bainbridge Island today," he says. "Later, if there's time and you two have the energy, we'll walk along Green Lake."

"Is that what you're wearing?" Shelly asks.

"Nah," Theo chuckles. "It's too cold on the ferry to go *au naturel.*"

Shelly's eyes follow him as Theo pours himself a cup of coffee. "Pot may be legal here, but public nudity isn't." He winks.

I slip past Theo to use the toilet.

After we all dress, Theo and I straighten up the living room from last night while Shelly makes peanut butter sandwiches for lunch. We fill our water bottles and I bring the bag of grapes I bought in the underground grocery.

It's a warm day, but Theo warns us to bring jackets. "It gets cold out on the water." He looks at Shelly's feet. As usual, she's wearing flip flops. "You should change into walking shoes, Val."

She huffs at him.

"Yeah, those things offer no support," I say. She glares at me.

"We're going to do a lot of walking today," Theo adds.

Shelly places her hands on her hips and pouts. "I hate you both." She changes into a bright yellow pair of Nikes.

As we walk toward the bus stop, she says, "My next boyfriend won't be such a shoe Nazi."

Theo and I give each other the high five, but these 'next boyfriend' remarks are wearing thin.

The bus drops us off near the waterfront. "Have you ever been on a ferry?" Theo asks me.

"No. The only kind of boat I've been on is a fishing boat."

Theo smiles and slaps me on the back. "You're in for a treat."

We buy tickets and wait to board.

Right before we set sail, a deep tone blares from the boat. Theo leans across the rail. "I never tire of that sound. A sea journey is an ancient rite, a timeless act that defies other modes of transport. Car and jet travel have their charms, but nothing beats a boat."

"Are we free to roam about?" I ask.

Theo nods. "Another way in which sea travel is superior to the air."

The ferry pulls away from the dock and the engine thunders beneath us.

"Does this scare you?" Shelly asks me.

"Not at all. There's plenty of land around us, and if I had to, I could swim ashore."

"I'd pay to see that."

I gaze at the grayish water. Shelly sidles up and I wrap my arms around her.

"I'm going to find the men's room," Theo says. "You kids behave."

When he's out of earshot, Shelly asks, "So what do you think of Theo?"

"He's not what I expected."

"I think he likes you," she says. "You're the little brother he never had."

"Is he an only child?"

"No. He has an older brother and a sister."

Her intimate access to Theo's history slices through me. She probably even knows his favorite brand of underwear.

The ferry draws further from the shore and the temperature drops. We zip up our jackets and put on our hoods.

When Theo comes back, he asks, "Want to go explore the ship? The upper deck has an even better view."

As I climb the metal staircase I grip the handrail, unsteady in the wind. The draft blows my hood off, and Shelly snaps a picture of me with my hair standing straight out.

"Give me your phone." Shelly takes another pic of me with my phone, then hands our phones to Theo. "Take obnoxious tourist shots of me and Michael."

A woman nearby offers to photograph all three of us with Bainbridge Island in the background.

Once ashore, the boat takes a few minutes to dock. A worker releases the rope holding passengers back, and we all file off the boat. "What should we do now?" Shelly asks.

"There's not much *to* do here," Theo says, and shrugs. "Sometimes I just ride the ferry over and turn around and go right back for fun."

"Do you want to do that now?" Shelly says.

"We'd have more time at Green Lake."

The three of us stroll near the dock and sit at a nearby picnic table and eat our sandwiches as we wait for a return ferry. "Too bad it's so expensive to live on these islands," Theo says. "This would be a perfect place to write."

"Wouldn't you get bored?" I say, thinking about how dull it is in Rooster.

"I'd take the ferry into town if I needed stimulation. One of the problems with being a writer in Seattle is the endless distractions."

When we make it back across to the city, we catch a bus heading north toward Green Lake, which has a three-mile walking path.

It's after ten o'clock when we return to Theo's, and Dale has already left for work. The three of us are too tired for another all-night conversation.

I slip off my clothes, toss them on the floor, and sit on the edge of the mattress wearing only boxers. "I suspect he's intentionally wearing us out so we don't do any monkey business in his bed."

"Monkey business?" Shelly slides out of her jeans and kicks them aside.

"You know what I mean." I wriggle my eyebrows up and down and give her my most seductive grin.

She laughs and straddles me. "No. You're going to have to show me, Prince Flynnstone of Mikelandia."

I kiss her and pull off her T-shirt. She places her hand on my chest and pushes me back on the mattress.

Chapter Seventeen
Michael

The shower is running again when I wake and I assume Theo's in there. But when I pull on my boxers and step out of the bedroom, I notice him reading in a chair. I peek behind the shower curtain, hoping it's not Dale. "Want some company?"

"Get in here." A hand reaches out and pulls me into the tub as I slip out of my underwear.

"Hello," I say, "Come here often?"

She giggles. "As often as I can."

The warm spray drenches me and Shelly lathers my head with shampoo. Soap bubbles slide down her body and I glide my sudsy fingers over her flesh as if polishing a precious stone. Our lips meet and we plunge into the ocean, deeper and deeper, knowing soon we'll need to come up for air. Yet we linger, and I am a bear scavenging her flesh, her soft curves against my rigid bones, my lips on her skin. I want her to climb me like a ladder and carry her with me until time stops.

The water eventually runs cold and we're transported back to reality.

There's only one clean towel and we share it to dry off. I slide my boxers back on as Shelly wraps up in the towel.

"I'm going to dry my hair," she says.

"Okay. I'll go get dressed."

She faces the mirror and combs through her wet strands. I pull her toweled torso against mine and kiss her neck. "I'm going to miss you."

"It will only take about five minutes to do my hair."

"You know what I mean."

She turns, and we kiss. When we finally separate, she rests her wet head on my chest. "I'm going to miss you, too, Neruda." She pushes back. "But you need to go away so I can fix my hair."

I dress and follow the aroma of coffee. A glance out the window shows gray sky and rain. With a cup of coffee in hand, I move into the living room. Theo and I nod at one another, and I join him in the adjacent chair. I set my cup on the floor.

"So, did you two leave me any hot water?" he asks.

I give him a sheepish grin, and change the subject. "I didn't know you wore glasses."

Theo touches the edge of his frames. "I have a slight astigmatism, and when I read a lot, they help." He sets his book down. "How are you feeling about the workshop?"

"Do you mean am I nervous?" I scratch my chin, wondering if I should shave today. "Kind of. I have no idea what to expect."

"You seem to be handling everything with great calm."

"My wacked out life prepared me for one bizarre event after another. I'm like a twenty-first century Odysseus."

Theo curls his lip, studies me. "Here's one more Homeric complication. I looked over my class list, and it turns out I'm your fiction instructor. If that's going to be awkward, we can switch you to Brian or Cody's class."

I reach for my cup. "Might as well keep it weird."

Theo chuckles. "Good. I'd like to read your work."

The bathroom door squeaks open and Shelly emerges still wearing the towel, her black hair dried perfectly straight. She walks over and sits on my lap. Knowing she is nude under the cloth gives me a slight tremor. I wonder what Theo's thinking. Yeah, having him as my instructor won't be the least bit awkward.

"What do you want to do on our last day together, Neruda?" Shelly lifts the coffee mug from my hand and drinks from it.

I bury my face in her freshly shampooed hair. I love when she doesn't stink of cigarettes. "Whatever you want."

"You guys are on your own today." Theo indicates the books and folders at his feet. "I'm swamped."

"Whatever we do, it will have to be free or cheap," I say.

"Sculpture Park is free," Theo says. "It's on the waterfront a few blocks from where we picked up the ferry yesterday."

After Shelly dresses, we catch a bus downtown. She Googles the directions to Sculpture Park and reads the description of the park from her phone. "Built in 2007, Sculpture Park consists of three-point-four miles of walking paths that wander along the Seattle waterfront with panoramic views of the Space Needle, The Great Wheel, Elliot Bay and other attractions at the heart of the city."

We get off the bus at Third and Pine and follow Shelly's GPS. "There it is," she says, pointing to a tall white thing near the entrance.

"Looks like a giant white turd."

Shelly shoves me. "Stop being such a teenage boy."

"But I *am* a teenage boy."

"Then man up."

I laugh, and try to grab her, but she skitters away.

Near us stands a fountain where two cast iron figures face each another. One is a small boy, the other a man. Their hands reach out toward one another but they are stopped by distance, and the man and the boy alternate being swallowed by water.

Shelly takes my hand and we stroll inside the park. She guides me to a railing that separates land from water. We lean on it, and the sun inches out from the clouds, forming a glaze over the roiling water. Shelly tries to hold her hair down from the wind. "I don't know why I bothered to dry it. I'm sure I look like Medusa."

"I've always had a soft spot for girls with snakes in their hair." I tilt her chin and pull her face into mine. Her hair tangles around us, and I'm happy to be caught in her net. The world is just the two of us, the slap of water against the shore as our soundtrack.

The low moan of a ship's horn separates us, and we resume walking.

We snap some selfies with Puget Sound in the background. Shelly tells me to take a picture of her where it looks like she's climbing The Space Needle.

We walk further and Shelly points to a leaning, wheel-like structure with long blue spikes erupting from the top. "What the heck is *this*?"

"*That,*" I say, "is a typewriter eraser. How impressed are you that I know that?"

She huffs. "I can always depend on you as a fount of useless knowledge."

I take a selfie looking contemplative next to the giant eraser. It's nearly three times taller than me. "Here's something *else* I know. Male squids turn white when they fight one another, but when a male meets a female, he only shows the female his darker, gentler side."

She squints at me. "Is that some weird biological knowledge you inherited from your father?"

"No. It was in my biology text last quarter."

"Why would you remember that, though?"

I shrug. "I thinks it's a metaphor for why females are attracted to us dark, brooding types."

She rolls her eyes. "You're such a freak."

"Takes one to know one." I try to take her hand but she skirts my grasp. As we continue to stroll we're dwarfed by a series of red walls.

At the visitor's center, when Shelly comes out of the restroom, she spots me reading a brochure. She leans over my shoulder. "Whatcha looking at?"

"Facts about what we've seen. Remember that father and son sculpture at the entrance?" She nods. "According to this, "it portrays an impossible and poignant situation as the two face each other with arms outstretched, striving to overcome a seemingly insurmountable divide."

"That's so sad," she says.

I return the map to the slot. "It's the story of my life."

"He'll contact you," Shelly says. "Did you check your email this morning?"

"Nope." I take her hand and kiss it. "I wanted today to be all about you."

"Awwww. Now I feel bad about having bitchy thoughts about you earlier."

"It's your nature. One of the things I love about you is your bitchiness."

She links her arm with mine and we go back outside.

I should be enjoying this day, but as each minute ticks by, I'm reminded that soon, Shelly and I will be like two bottles in the sea carrying messages to separate oceans.

I kiss the top of her head. "I'm going to miss you the way the sun misses the moon when night becomes day."

"Are you getting all maudlin on me?"

"Yeah. What of it?" I bring her hand to my lips and taste her fingers. "I'm going to miss you as the sea misses the sand at low tide."

Shelly extracts her hand from my grip. "It's not like we'll never see each other again, Neruda."

I grab her waist and squeeze her tighter. "I've gotten used to you pestering me every day, telling me where to be and what time to be there. I won't survive on my own."

"Yes, you will." She pulls away. "You need to fly, baby bird, fly."

I walk backwards, flapping my arms. "I did fly. All the way from Ohio." My foot slips and I stumble onto the damp earth.

Shelly squeals and collapses on top of me. "How *will* you survive without me?"

I roll us over and pin her down on the wet grass. "I won't. You need to stow away in the dorm with me and protect me from myself."

"Two weeks in a beach front hotel on Maui versus a skanky dorm?" She shoves me off and sits up. "Some choice."

I stand, pull her up, and we finish the walk. My steps are intentionally slow.

After we circle back to the waterfront entrance I avoid looking at the father and son sculpture. Shelly and I dip into a small coffee shop near the park and I treat her to a latte and a pizza-sized peanut butter cookie.

We carry our coffees outside and sit on a bench overlooking Elliot Bay. I set my drink on the concrete near my feet and lean into myself, resting my face on top of my fist.

"What's the matter, Neruda? You look like that Thinker statue."

"The insurmountable divide between *us* looms."

She curls her hands around my arm and rests her head on my shoulder. "But exciting things are about to happen. You have that writing gig, and your father is somewhere around the corner." She points at a man who looks to be a hundred and fifty-years-old hobbling toward us. "Look! That could be him right now."

I glance up briefly. "Ha! Nice try."

She bites into her enormous cookie and holds it up for me. I mangle a large chunk of it, chew, and resume my pensive pose.

"What do you want from me, Neruda?"

"I need you to guarantee I'm not about to screw up my life."

She loops her arm around my shoulder. "I can't guarantee I won't screw up my own life, more less yours."

"And I want you to say you'll miss me, too."

"You know I will."

"Then why do I feel like you're drawing away from me?"

Shelly sighs. "Everything ends eventually."

"Including us?"

Shelly bites her lip and does not respond.

We sit quietly, watching the sun and clouds battle for attention. Part of me knows I've already lost her. I can trap Shelly inside a cage or handcuff her to my side, but one of the things I love about her is she chooses her own way.

Clouds win the weather war and we drift back to Theo's under drizzling rain.

I pack my bag and Shelly walks with me to the university to check in. We follow signs marked "HHSOW Registration" to find the Communications building.

At the front steps, she says, "I should probably let you do the rest of this on your own."

"I'm in no hurry."

"You need to fly, baby bird," she says again.

I flap my arms at her but she won't look at me. We embrace for a long time, and then she backs away.

"Last chance to stow away," I say.

She runs her hands along my face as if reading braille. "This is the part of the story where the heroine sets the hero free so he can conquer new worlds."

"Maybe this hero doesn't want his freedom. Maybe the hero likes being a prisoner of love."

"It's too late," she says. "The scene has already been written into our story."

"Give me a red pen and I'll delete that part."

Shelly smiles, but her eyes are sad. She kisses me, and turns to leave.

I grab her hand. "Maybe nothingness is to be without your presence…."

She places two fingers on my lips and shakes her head. "Please, don't quote Neruda to me. You know he makes me cry, and that can't be good for either of us today."

I strain to delay her exit. "Will you be at the reading tonight?"

"Of course." She lets me hold her hand against my chest so I can kiss her fingertips before finally releasing her.

Chapter Eighteen
Michael

The guy at the sign-in table hands me a room key, a campus map, and a canvas tote bag. "Inside you'll find your schedule and some other handouts. What size T-shirt do you wear?"

"Medium."

He reaches into a box marked Men's Medium and hands me a crimson colored T-shirt with HHSOW emblazoned in white letters on the front. "They want you to wear this to dinner tonight." He stretches his arm to the right. "Your dorm is two buildings that way."

I heave my suitcase and backpack up to the third floor and find my room. My roommate's stuff is strewn across the mattress of the lower bunk, but he's not here. I wheel my suitcase against the wall and lob my backpack onto the top bunk.

The room contains two fiberboard desks, two stiff wooden chairs, the bunk beds, two small dressers, and a wardrobe. Each bed is topped with a pillow, a set of sheets and towels, and a single blue blanket folded in a stack. A north facing window provides light, but little comfort.

Since my roommate has chosen a bed, I select the desk closest to the window. I unzip my pack and stack my notebooks on the desktop. I slide my pens and highlighter inside the single drawer.

There are no hangers in the wardrobe. Crap. Do we have to buy those, too? For almost a year I lived out of cardboard boxes in the back seat of my car, so living out of a suitcase won't be anything new. The only thing worth hanging up is my Hawaiian shirt, which I wrap across the back of my desk chair. The shirt always reminds me of the day Shelly kidnapped me for our first real date. It's also the shirt I'm wearing in my fake ID photo.

I stash my second pair of running shoes on the floor under the desk and look at my home for the next three weeks. I am alone and this room confirms it.

I load the campus map, a small notebook, and a couple of pens in my side pocket.

The campus bookstore teems with people; clusters of them already wearing the red shirts, yet their presence amplifies my loneliness. I find a ridiculously high-priced, cheap-ass desk lamp and a used paperback thesaurus.

As I wait in line to pay, images of Shelly click through my head—her bawdy laugh, her intensity, those damned cigarettes stinking up my car, the softness of her hands, the softness of her neck, her hair, her hard yet supple soul.

Now I imagine Theo and Shelly alone together for the next two days. Will they revisit their history? She had said, "This is where the heroine sets the hero free." Does she want to be free?

A voice from behind me says, "Dude, are you going to just stand there?"

"Oh. Sorry." I move up to the register and pay with the credit card Earl and Dot gave me the day I flew out. "Just don't use it on strip clubs and hookers," Earl had said. "And don't make an ass of yourself, kid."

So far so good, Earl.

Back in the dorm, my roommate has come and gone. On the other desk sits a UW bookstore shopping bag and a sweatshirt draped across the back of the second chair.

I plug in my new desk lamp and turn it on. Shit. It didn't come with a bulb.

My phone buzzes. It's my sister. "Hey, Annie."

"Hi! How do you like Seattle?"

"It's cool. Just moved into the dorm."

"Jeff told me you know about Mom's arm," she says.

"Yeah. How's she handling it?"

"She's kind of cranky, especially since the cast is on her smoking hand. But the good news is Paul got her to clean all the crap off the steps."

"She threw stuff out?"

Annie sighs. "No, she moved it to my old room. Like I'd ever live there again."

"Some things never change."

"That's why you should never come back here."

My sister and I share a moment of silence. I'd like to think of Rooster as home, even though I was homeless there. "Hey, while I have you on the phone, I need to ask you something about girls."

"Girls have boobies and boys have pee pees," she replies in a mock teacher voice.

"I know *that*, nimrod. Seriously, though. It's about dating. I need to ask a girl, and you're the closest thing I can come up with."

Over the phone she gives me the raspberry. "Okay, I'm listening."

I prop my elbow on the desk and rest my chin in my palm. "When girls date a guy, are they always looking for who's next on the horizon? I mean, do they only stay until something better comes along?"

"Do you think Shelly is seeing someone else?"

I scrunch my brow. "No, but she keeps making comments like, "the next guy I date will be like this or that. I *think* she's kidding, but I'm not so sure."

"Hmmm. Has she *said* she wants to break up?"

"Not outright." I drum my fingers on the desktop. "But she's never asked me to go to Baltimore with her. In fact, she's sort of pushing me to stay out here."

"She flew out to Seattle with you, so I don't think she's trying to dump you."

"Maybe. Maybe not. But I also have the feeling she came here partly to see her old flame, who, by the way, is far too good-looking."

"*How* good looking?"

"Way more than I'm comfortable with. Picture Brad Pitt or Chris Hemsworth."

"Awwwww. It sucks to be you, doesn't it?"

"Totally."

"Just ask her. Say, 'Shelly, are you trying to break up with me?'"

"I try, but she always says, 'I don't want to talk about that right now.'"

Annie pauses. "Not all high school couples stay together. When we read Romeo and Juliet last year, our teacher said all love stories end tragically."

I massage the back of my neck. "Great. That helps a lot."

"Sorry. Hey, have you heard from your father yet?"

"Not a peep."

The door opens and a suntanned guy who looks as if he'd be comfortable riding a surf board-steps in.

"Hey, listen, Annie, I gotta go. I'll text or email you later. Love you."

"Love you, too."

The guy holds out his hand to me. "Hunter Perry."

We shake hands. "Michael G. Flynn." I started adding the G to deflect from the well-known criminal by that name.

"Welcome to our palatial paradise."

I chuff a laugh. This guy doesn't know I've lived in smaller accommodations.

Hunter unpacks his stuff, and after he hangs up his shirts, he gives me the rest of his hangers. "They come in packs of twelve, and I only need eight."

"Thanks." I hang up the Hawaiian shirt along with a couple of T-shirts.

Hunter plops down on his bed. "I see you bought a desk lamp."

"Yeah, but I forgot to buy a bulb."

"There's a drugstore not too far away. They have other supplies, too. Cheaper than the campus store."

"I'll check it out."

"We have a little time before dinner. I'll walk you over there and show you where it is."

"Sure, why not?" Nothing better to do.

When we step outside, Hunter asks, "Where are you from?"

"Rooster, Ohio. How about you?"

"Malibu."

"So, what made you apply for the workshop?"

"Writing's sort of in my family blood," Hunter says. "My parents are screenwriters, so I grew up around story. I've been accepted at CCU in the film school. I'm hoping this program gives me a jump start." He looks at me. "How about you? What brought you here?"

There are a thousand ways to answer that question, but I don't know Hunter at all, so I stuff my hands in my pockets, and say, "It sounded kind of cool."

We turn a corner and head toward a row of stores. Bartell Drugs is half a block ahead.

"They sell beer here, too," Hunter says. "I'm planning to buy a mini fridge."

"Good to know," I respond, hoping he doesn't ask me to go in halves with him. A couple of girls wearing the red shirts and carrying the tote bags walk ahead of us. "Are we supposed to carry those bags around?"

"I think that's optional. We need to wear the red T-shirts tonight, though."

Inside the drugstore I buy a two-pack of bulbs, some gum, and a can of Pringles. Hunter also buys junk food and we walk back to the dorm. We change into our red shirts, and head to the conference center for the opening reception.

"No offense," Hunter says, "but we'll see each other every day, so I'm going to sit at a different table and meet new people." He taps my shoulder and ambles to a table near the center of the room. I envy his social ease.

All the tables are round with white tablecloths, a salad and water glass at each place setting. I spot two open seats at a table near the back. "Are these seats taken?" The others shake their heads.

Theo's sitting near the front with other adults. He's wearing a well-fitting khaki shirt, and talking amiably with an attractive blonde woman, his arm resting behind her chair. Maybe nothing will happen between him and Shelly. Maybe I can talk Shelly into coming back to the dorm with me after the reading. We can sleep outside somewhere on the grass like we did one night shortly before graduation. The day had been unbearably hot, and Shelly and I took a drive in The Whale out to the boonies to cool our bones. Thinking of The Whale now stabs me in the chest. Is it weird to miss a car?

But on that day, after buying tomatoes and peaches at a fruit stand, we headed to one of the locks where there are camping areas. Homeless people know where all the safe camp grounds are, and when I lived in my car, I ventured out there occasionally. I still keep blankets in the back from when I lived in it, so that night we spread them on the grass. As it grew dark, Shelly and I decided to stay the night. I texted Annie, knowing she'd tell Earl and Dot, and Shelly texted her Mom.

Even though there were other campers nearby, nobody bothered us, and it was just me and Shelly under the stars. We watched lightning bugs flicker and fell asleep in each other's arms.

The guy next to me at the table interrupts my thoughts. "What's your chief genre?"

I turn, and reply, "fiction. How about you?"

"Poetry." He extends his hand. "My name's Brad Xu." His voice is deep, and he sounds more like a forty-year-old white man than a thin, young Asian in a baggy T-shirt. "Everyone calls me Shoe."

"Michael G. Flynn." We shake hands, and I give a probing glance at Shoe's enormous shirt, which falls around him like a dress.

Shoe grins. "By the time I checked in all they had left were men's 2 XL."

A bearded man stands at the podium and suddenly the room grows quiet. He introduces himself as the program director.

"Welcome students, staff, and teachers to the second annual Hugo House Summer of Writing. Tonight's dinner is our gift to you. Enjoy the setting and the food because from here on out your meals will be in the dining hall, and the food and ambience will be far less appetizing." There's a scatter of laughter throughout.

"As writers we should be reading and writing outside our comfort zones. It forces us to become better writers. Just as some of you suffered through physics and calculus in high school, you will stretch your writing muscles by exploring other disciplines within the creative realm." He pauses for a second and shuffles his notes.

"I won't kid you; you will work hard this summer, and sometimes it will hurt, yet ultimately, you'll enjoy the process. We'll discuss the finer points of your schedules and other housekeeping at tomorrow's orientation. Tonight, enjoy your meal, talk to people at your tables. I'll see you at the reading later."

After dinner, I walk with Shoe and a couple of our tablemates to the auditorium for the reading. On the way, we encounter a guy whose T-shirt is too snug and he and Shoe trade shirts.

At the entrance to the auditorium, I say, "I'm going to wait for my girlfriend."

Shelly is chatting with Theo and a blonde woman. The trio suddenly erupts in laughter, and this grieves me. She belongs to others now.

Then she locks her gaze on me, and for a moment, the world is righted again.

Shelly and I sit with my dinner companions in the middle section. I reach over to hold her hand but she's texting. I sneak a peek at the screen, but she tilts her phone away.

"Texting your next boyfriend?"

She elbows me. "Shut up."

The program director introduces each of the teachers, and they read either a poem or an excerpt from a longer piece. When Theo approaches the podium, Shelly leans in and whispers, "he's going to read a scene from his dissertation about our San Francisco experience."

Her use of 'our' digs through me, reminding me she will be alone with him for the next two nights. My attention is heightened as Theo narrates a piece about his and Shelly's attempts to find a motel without bed bugs. In the essay he calls her Valentine.

As we stride out of the auditorium, I grip Shelly's free hand. We stand at the bottom of the steps in the pink light of dusk. It's a perfect summer night, the kind of night when, as a kid, I stayed outdoors way past bed time because the light and temperature were impeccable. My mother's face was a moonlit miracle, and she laughed every time Jeff and I smacked each other with pool noodles, pretending they were light sabers. If I were still seven years-old, I would want to do just that at this moment.

I'm no longer a kid, and right now I'd like to pull Shelly away from this crowd, lean her against a dark corner of the building and cover her in kisses, but I detect a wintry energy coming from her, so I do nothing.

"What's next?" I ask.

She bites her lip. "Wait for Theo, I guess."

Theo strides out of the building with the blonde from dinner, who is also one of the poetry instructors. After a minute, she pecks Theo on the cheek and walks away. Theo sees Shelly and me, waves, and trots down the steps in our direction.

"I don't *have* to stay in the dorm tonight," I say. "I could walk back with you guys. Or you and I could grab the blanket off my bed and go sleep on the green. There's a real nice fountain..."

Shelly places a hand on my chest. "I think it's better if you stay here."

"Why?"

"You need to make friends."

"I've got three weeks to make new friends. We won't see each other for a long time."

She rolls her eyes. "Neruda, you'll see me Sunday when you take me to the airport."

"You know what I mean."

Theo reaches the bottom step. "Did you guys enjoy the reading?"

Shelly extracts her hand from my chest. "Your story was the best, of course."

Theo snorts. "You have to say that because you're my houseguest."

Shelly glances at me and my jaw tightens.

Theo eyeballs us. "I'll give you two a minute." He steps away and pulls out his phone to make a call.

"I won't keep you, seeing as how you can't *wait* to get away from me."

"Michael, don't be like that." She reaches for me, but I shake her off. She sighs. "I'll see you Sunday, okay? You'll come by around noon?"

"I'll be there." I stuff my hands in my pockets and stalk away.

Out of the corner of my eye, I watch Theo and Shelly stroll toward Theo's apartment. I want to trust her, but those two have shared entire chapters that don't include me.

Back to the dorm I hear raucous laughter coming from my room. Hunter has already made friends with some guys and they're crowded into our room. "We're trying to devise a plan for scoring some alcohol," Hunter says.

"This is your lucky day, gentlemen." I reach for my wallet, and flash the fake ID. "According to this, I'm twenty-two-year-old Michael Neruda."

"Awesome, dude." Hunter gives me a fist bump. "I knew I liked you."

Chapter Nineteen
Shelly

Shelly watches Michael stuff his hands in his pockets and stalk away. When Theo comes back from his phone call, she says, "if you and Flora want to get together tonight, I can get a hotel room."

"Don't be silly. I can see her every day. You, on the other hand, are a rare bird."

Shelly links her arm in his and they walk toward his place. "Feels like old times."

"Minus the bed bugs."

One of the things Shelly likes about Theo is his easy confidence. She feels protected when she's with him. With Michael, Shelly usually takes the lead.

Back at his apartment he pours the remainder of last night's wine into two glasses. They chat for a few minutes, and he says, "I hate to be a rude host, but I need to prepare my class notes."

"That's fine," Shelly says. "I can read one of the books I bought." At Left Bank Books she picked up *Hillbilly Elegy*. She didn't let Michael see her buy it. He may have gotten annoyed, but Shelly thought the book might help her understand Michael's origins.

"Tomorrow I'll take you to the Farmer's Market in Ballard. It's awesome."

"Looking forward to it."

Theo flips his stereo on and the blues play from the speakers. The apartment is so small Shelly hears it clearly in the bedroom.

She props the pillows against the wall and begins to read her book.

Blue Valentines by Tom Waits comes on the radio. That song makes her think of Michael and the time they dangled their feet in her pool and sang along.

Maybe she should have taken Michael up on his offer to spend one more night together. But his neediness got on her nerves and she couldn't wait to get away from him. Now, as she rests on Theo's mattress, she misses Michael's physical presence.

She wraps the sheet around her shoulders. It still smells of Michael and his earthy aroma. Michael worries so much about body odor he always wears cologne. She grins, remembering how he used to hoard samples of expensive cologne he tore from magazines.

Shelly tosses the book aside and goes to the living room. "Do you have any more wine?"

Theo looks up from his papers. "I always have wine." He sets his papers down and retreats to the kitchen to open a new bottle of Cabernet Sauvignon.

Chapter Twenty
Michael

My new buddies and I are all still buzzed during the morning orientation. After lunch, we stop at a guy named Reed's room so he can get his car keys. Reed scored a solo room at the end of the hall since his roommate dropped at the last minute.

Hunter found a used mini fridge for sale and we're going to go pick it up.

Dave, Hunter, and I pile into Reed's car, a brand-new BMW 335i. It's a midnight blue convertible with white leather interior. "Nice wheels," I say. This isn't even the same species as The Blue Whale.

"Thanks," Reed says. "Texas oil money."

As we cruise around in Reed's car, deciding what to do after we drop the fridge at the dorm, Dave lights a joint.

Hunter looks at his phone. "The Gay Pride parade is today. Let's go."

By the time Reed finds somewhere to park, the parade is underway. We follow the noise to where masses of people line the street. There's a thrum of energy accompanied with shouting, whooping, and singing. People wear tie-dyed shirts in bright colors, and the thump thump thump of a bass drum comes from a band led by a group holding rainbow flags. I text Shelly twice but she doesn't respond.

A guy next to us says, "look, there's George Takei!" And there he is, an older version of Sulu from *Star Trek*, five feet away. He's followed by a group of cowboys wearing sleeveless rainbow shirts with ties.

"This is awesome," I say. "I'm definitely not in Rooster, Ohio anymore.

As floats drive by the participants toss things to the crowd. I snap a selfie with a group of guys in drag wearing feathered headdresses and text it to Shelly. I stare at my phone, expecting a sarcastic response, but all I get is silence.

Chapter Twenty-One
Michael

I drag myself up for a couple miles' run before breakfast. I need to sweat out the beer, weed, and sadness. Last night I loosened up enough to dance. But I haven't heard from Shelly since Friday night.

The day is gloomy and the wind is cold, a perfect match for my mood.

Hunter is still asleep after I return from my run. I shower, quietly dress, and head to the dining hall. Still queasy from last night, I fill my plate with a stack of toast and something that resembles sausage. I already miss Dot's breakfasts of fresh eggs, homemade biscuits, and crispy bacon. They have eggs and bacon here, but the eggs have no flavor and the bacon is flaccid. I fill two cups with black coffee and set those on the tray and look for a table.

Shoe, the guy with the deep voice from dinner Friday, is the only familiar face. We nod a greeting, and I place my tray next to his.

"Looks like today's our final day of rest before the work begins," he says.

"Guess so." I take a giant slug of coffee. "How do you plan to spend it?"

"I haven't decided. There's a couple of bookstores nearby Maybe I'll check out. You're welcome to join me."

"I would, but I'm seeing my girlfriend off to the airport later." I *assume* she's still my girlfriend.

"Is she the one who sat with us at the reading the other night?"

"Yep. That's Shelly."

"She's pretty," he says. "How long have you two been together?"

"A year." I swig more coffee. "We met while doing community service together. How about you? Do you have a girl back home?"

He nods. "Sort of. We've been dating since we were juniors."

I don't usually reveal personal stuff with just anyone but something about Shoe feels okay. Maybe it's his sage old voice. Or maybe I'm so far out of my comfort zone I reveal the whole freak show about how, a year ago, I was expelled for bringing fireworks to school.

"With the intent of blowing up my ex-best friend's car, not the school," I add. "My sentence was spending last summer cleaning up the high school. Shelly also had a list of crimes and misdemeanors, including smoking in school, car theft, and running away to California with a guy she met on the Internet. Her parents didn't press charges for stealing one of their cars, but they wanted her to suffer, so they made her help clean the school all summer."

I don't tell Shoe the guy from the Internet is Theo in case he also has him for a class.

"That's an amazing story," he says. "I envy your experiences. The most interesting thing I've ever done is take a whizz off the water tower in my hometown."

I crack up. "That's great, though. I'd never have the nerve for that. I'm not a big fan of heights."

"It was a metaphor for 'piss on you' to the town during graduation week. None of us plans to go back there when we finish college."

"A lot of kids escape my town, too."

We compare schedules and learn we're in the same poetry and fiction workshops. "So how did you learn about the program?" I ask.

"My guidance counselor told me about it. She knew I planned to major in creative writing at Bennington. My parents were hesitant since Washington is so far away from home."

"Where are you from?"

"Picnic Pines, Maine.

"That sounds even smaller than Rooster, Ohio."

Shoe chuckles. "We have about twelve thousand people. Most are connected to the local college. How about your town?"

"Twenty-five thousand or so. There's a couple of nearby colleges, but a lot of people in town barely finish high school."

"My parents are both physics professors," he says. "I'm the token weirdo in the family. The rebel poet."

"And your parents don't mind?"

"Luckily, I have a brother and sister who will fulfill the obligatory math and science careers expected of Asian students." He slabs jelly on his toast. "Wouldn't it be ironic if *I'm* the one to win a Nobel Prize?"

We part company after eating. I stop at the dorm, but Hunter is gone. We've only been here a couple of days, but the room is starting to smell like my mother's house. I gather up the stray beer cans and junk food bags and toss them in a trash bag. We're supposed to recycle the cans, but I want all this crap out of my room. I crack the window open and dump the trash bag at the end of the hall.

It's only eleven, but I've got nothing better to do, so I grab my pack and head over to Theo's. As I walk, visions of Theo and Shelly chasing each other naked in his living room loop through my head. Yeah, I over-think everything.

Shelly answers the door and I'm relieved she's fully clothed, wearing a short aqua blue dress. Her damp hair is braided and dangling across one shoulder. "Hey."

"Hey." I step inside the apartment. "Where's Theo?"

"In the shower."

"I came early. Hope it's not a problem."

"I'm all packed, but I want to say goodbye to Theo first."

"Sure. I get that."

I would sit, but both chairs are covered with books and papers. Shelly wheels her big suitcase out of Theo's bedroom. That confirms where *she* slept last night. From the looks of the living room, I'm not sure Theo slept in *here*, though.

"That's quite a suitcase," I say.

Shelly glances at the brightly patterned luggage with yellow, orange, and pink flowers on a green background. "You saw it when we flew out."

I shrug. "I think I was too busy envisioning my impending death from a fiery plane crash to notice."

"My mom bought it for the Hawaii trip. She thought it looked tropical."

"Well, you'll never have to worry about me borrowing it."

"Ha ha."

I tug Shelly into my arms. "I'm going to miss you, Shelly Bean."

Shelly rests her head on my chest. "I'll miss you, too, Neruda."

The shower clicks off, and less than a minute later, a towel clad Theo emerges. Shelly breaks from my embrace.

Theo looks slightly surprised. "Good morning, Michael."

"Morning," I reply.

Theo ruffles through his wet hair. His torso flexes like a guy on a romance book cover. Shelly looks away.

"Are you psyched and ready for tomorrow?" Theo asks me.

"Getting there."

"We'd better get going," Shelly says.

Theo extends his arms to her and she steps into them. "Keep in touch, *Valentina*." He kisses the top of her head and they share a hug I'm not comfortable with, especially considering he's only wearing a towel. Shelly finally backs away. I follow her out the door, banging her suitcase down the steps.

Shelly suggests we eat lunch and we find a Subway nearby.

"Have you made any friends?" Shelly asks, as we sit down with our food.

"Yeah." I rip open a bag of chips. "Michael F. Neruda made a bunch of new friends because he can buy beer and marijuana."

"You brought your ID! Smart."

I tell her about Hunter and how he and some other guys scored a mini fridge and got shitfaced Friday and Saturday nights.

"Is that all you do in the dorms?" She stabs at her salad with a plastic fork. "Get drunk and stoned?"

"No. Yesterday we went to a Gay Pride parade, and then we crashed a party. I actually danced."

She raises her hands as if to pray. "Please tell me there's video."

I steal a couple of her Fritos. "I texted you a picture last night. In fact, I've sent you several texts."

"Oh! I had my phone plugged into the charger in Theo's kitchen."

"The whole weekend?"

She pulls out her phone and smiles. "There you are." She turns it so I can see the photo of me grinning like an idiot next to a drag queen wearing a feathered headdress. She sets the phone on the table. "You should email it to your father so he knows what you look like."

I snort. "Hey, Dad, I'm your long-lost gay son. Be my daddy!"

Shelly crunches and swallows some salad. "Have you heard from him yet?"

"Nope." I remove the lid and take a swig of Coke. "I'd almost forgotten about him. I'm hoping maybe my message went into his spam."

She spears me with a look. "Michael, the primary reason you're here is to meet him."

I crush a couple of potato chips with my thumb. "I'm not so sure that's a good idea."

"Why?"

"Everything about being here is unsettling. It's as if I'm walking the plank into a shark filled ocean and the closest lifeboats are hundreds of miles away."

She reaches out and takes my hands. "We've worked too hard to get you here."

"*You* got me here. This whole freak show was your idea."

"Yes, but you got into the workshop on your merits." She draws her hands away and sips her Diet Coke. "Michael, don't blow this chance to meet your father."

"I may not have time anyway." I dig into my pocket and pull out a mangled schedule.

"You're going to be busy," she says. "You won't have much time to lead the life of a stoner."

"I know, and just when I was getting good at it." I wad up the sandwich wrapper and slurp the rest of my pop.

"Are you going to write about me?" Shelly asks.

"I told you I don't like to write about people I care about."

She swizzles the straw in her drink. "Maybe you should stop caring so much.*"*

I pop a few ice cubes into my mouth to chew. "So, what happened at Theo's after I moved into the dorm? What kept you so busy you couldn't bother to text me back?"

She gives me a coy smile. "What happens at Theo's stays at Theo's."

"That's not fair. I told you all about my drunken debauchery."

"I don't have to share every detail of my life with you."

I crush the rest of my chips with my fist. "You should know by now I have an overactive imagination. And a short fuse."

She stands and gathers her trash. "We'd better get going."

I wheel her suitcase behind me as we amble to the transit center. Near the platform Shelly looks up at me as I set her suitcase down. "Let's just say our goodbyes here. Avoid the messy, long drawn-out Hollywood adieu."

"But your flight doesn't leave for like three more hours."

She shrugs. "I just need to be alone right now."

"Maybe I'm not ready to say good-bye just yet."

"You'll forget me the moment you meet all those emo poetry chicks in your workshop." She slides her credit card in the ticket machine and pulls out her boarding pass.

"Shelly, I'm not looking to replace you."

"Maybe you should be."

I tighten my fists. "Why do you keep saying that? Is this part of your plan? To get me to Seattle and then abandon me?"

"Michael…." She turns her face away.

"Shit. That *was* your plan."

"Michael, you're a really good guy, but I think we need to keep our options open."

"Are you *breaking up* with me?"

"No. I don't know. Maybe. We're both headed in new directions and … and I'm one nut shy of peanut brittle."

I loosen my fingers and give her a melancholy smile. "I like peanut brittle. It's sweet and salty."

She reaches up and brushes my bangs out of my eyes. "Look, I…I just want to be me for a while."

I cup her face in my hands and kiss her forehead. "There's nobody like you, Shelly bean. You're my best friend."

Her voice grows thin as a reed. "And you're mine."

"Then why do you want us to split up?"

Shelly pulls away, looks down, and shakes her head. "I don't *want* to…"

"Are we still…us?"

She takes a long breath. "I think we're becoming us, 2.0. Just two people discovering who we are."

"That doesn't mean we have to break up."

She rests her head on my chest, and her voice shakes. "Let's not get all maudlin, Neruda. I just need to go."

I press her into me, and she lets me hold her, but the train pulls up and she jerks back. She doesn't look at my face.

"So, this is it? You just walk away and expect me to be fine with it?".

Shelly looks up, her eyes on the edge of tears. She reaches for the handle of her suitcase. "The only thing I expect is for you to understand."

"Well, I *don't*."

"You will." She steps back and rolls the flowered suitcase behind her. Then she stops and glances at me over her shoulder. "Let me know how the workshop is going. And meet your father."

"That might be out of my control."

"Send him another note or call the number on his web page." She gives me a sad grin and a short wave. "I'll text you when I get there." She boards the train and does not look back.

Soon the doors close and the train speeds away. Everything grows gray, as if Shelly snatched up all the colors and took them with her.

It starts pouring, so I hop on a bus that should get me back to campus. Rain pecks against the windows, providing a soundtrack for my sadness. This city is massive and bleak and I'm a solo act here. Would anyone here give a damn if this bus crashed and I didn't make it back to the dorm? Theo might notice one less student in his fiction workshop. Hunter would have more space for parties in our room.

Then there's my father. Ha! Wouldn't it be ironic if he replied to my message right after pieces of me were strewn across the streets of Seattle?

Nothing looks familiar, and I realize this bus is not headed to UW campus. I open my phone and look up my dorm. "Dammit!" I'll have to backtrack a couple of miles. Uphill. In the rain.

Getting lost isn't fatal. Just annoying. When I first learned how to drive I purposely got lost in order to find new ways around town. It came in handy once I was homeless.

As I pass a bus stop, I notice the acronym for public transportation here is ORCA. Now there's irony. Transitioning from The Blue Whale to using ORCA. Maybe I *am* destined to be here.

By the time I make it back to the room all I want to do is change into dry clothes, but our room is full of people. Hunter informs me we need to restock the mini fridge.

Hunter hands me a wad of cash for, "some chips and shit for study hall tonight." Study Hall is our euphemism for getting shitfaced.

It's still raining, so I don't bother to change clothes before walking to Bartell's.

After a tasteless dinner in the dining hall, a bunch of us meet in Dave Fry's room. Dave and a few others have also managed to score some beer and a bottle of Jack Daniels.

I'm already sick of alcohol, yet I stay long enough for two beers. I'd make a lousy alcoholic. My headstone will say *Michael G Flynn lacked the commitment to stay drunk.*

Finally, the rain stops, and I opt for some natural endorphins to smooth out my troubles. I change into running clothes and step outside.

A couple of girls I recognize from orientation are jogging ahead of me and I follow for a bit. One is tall, with extraordinary legs and a blonde ponytail, and the other is small-framed with dark, wavy hair. As much as I enjoy the view, they run too slowly for me, so I pass them and say, "How's it going?"

The next three weeks may not be so bad.

Chapter Twenty-Two
Shelly

Shelly walks into the terminal, her bright suitcase trailing behind her. Hawaii is her favorite vacation spot. And she should be excited, but she feels as if a strong wind blasted the joy out of her.

By the time she upgrades to First Class, checks her bag, and makes it through security, Shelly has two more hours before her flight boards. She stops at an airport bookstore and loads up on *People*, *Us*, and *Entertainment Weekly* magazines. Shelly finds the Delta Sky Lounge and stops in the lounge bathroom. She unleashes her hair from the braid and lets it fall in crinkled waves. She smears on red lipstick. Next, she uses her fake ID to score a glass of Merlot.

Shelly arrives at the gate just in time for First Class passenger boarding.

The flight attendant doesn't question her age and Shelly drinks another glass of wine. She skims through her magazines, which all feature couples. Is the entire world made up of couples? She stashes *People* and *Us* in the seat pocket. She should have bought *Scientific American* or *Business Week*.

The song *Blue Valentines* runs through her head like an ear worm. She thought she'd feel relief by breaking up with Michael, but things are unresolved. Why can't he accept they have no future? She orders a third glass of wine with her dinner. She eats a few bites and falls asleep before the attendant removes her tray.

It's after nine when she lands in Maui. She glances at her phone. Michael has sent her several sad and lonely texts.

She texts her brother.

-*I'm here!!!*

-*Cool. We're by the pool. Dad says to take the hotel limo.*

At the hotel a porter wearing a Hawaiian shirt accompanies Shelly to the suite she's sharing with Josh. She changes into shorts and a tank top and joins her family beside the hotel pool.

"Yay!" Josh jumps up and wraps his sister in a hug. "It's been dull as dirt without you here."

Their father laughs. "Says the son whose father is paying for his Ivy League tuition."

"Sorry, Dad, but you have to admit, you and Mom aren't the most stimulating company," Josh says, as he sits back down.

Mrs. Miller laughs and sips her drink.

"I spend all day being interesting at work," Mr. Miller says.

Mrs. Miller caresses her husband's face. "You've always been interesting to me."

Josh and Shelly look at one another and gag. Shelly notes the pitcher on the table filled with a hot pink liquid. "What are you drinking?"

"It's called a *wicked wahine*," Mrs. Miller says. "Pineapple juice, grenadine, and rum."

Shelly takes a sip of her mother's drink. "Mmmmmm. That's good."

"Knowing you'll find a way to obtain one anyway," Mr. Miller says. "I'm allowing you and your brother each one drink." He signals for a waiter to bring another glass for Shelly.

"Have you eaten dinner?" her mother asks.

"Not really." *Unless you count three glasses of wine.*

Mrs. Miller pushes a plateful of appetizers toward her.

The ocean sloshes nearby and her family looks golden lit by tiki torch light. Shelly picks up a coconut shrimp and dips it in a tangy sauce. None of it fills the void.

"You're being unnaturally quiet," Josh says.

"Am I?"

"I mean, I'm not complaining, but silence from you worries me."

Shelly sticks her tongue out at him. She plucks off the pineapple slice from the edge of her glass and eats it. "I think I broke up with Michael."

"You're not sure?"

"Well, I tried to end it, but he said no."

"Maybe a little time apart is the best thing for both of you," Mrs. Miller says. "You two have been inseparable since last summer."

"You'll be going to different colleges, so it's time to move on," Mr. Miller says.

"Yeah." But she can't get the image of his stricken face out of her mind, as if she'd dragged his body along a gravel highway. She opens her phone and looks at the photo he sent from the Gay Pride parade. The face she knows and loves.

After the snack and drink, Josh walks Shelly back to their room.

"Did you really dump Michael?"

She sighs. "I guess."

"Why did you choose him in the first place? He's not like anyone else you dated."

"Partly because he was so broken. He and I were mirrors, looking for lost pieces of ourselves."

"But now he's found his."

Shelly nods. "And mine is six feet under."

Josh stops. "Let me get this straight. Now that Michael is," he makes air quotes, "'whole,' you want to dump him?"

"No...I...it's hard to explain."

"Try me."

Shelly sits on a stone wall and Josh joins her. "It's like when you rescue a dying plant, and you water it and give it light. And after a while it blooms into this beautiful bouquet. That's what Michael is."

"Then why dump him?"

"He needs to bloom into different shapes and colors now. He won't fully flower if he feeds on the same soil."

Josh shakes his head. "Every plant you've tried to grow has died."

Shelly sighs. "Exactly."

Chapter Twenty-Three
Michael

The poetry professor stands at the front of room and scans our faces. "Who are you people?" Each of us turns to look at one another.

"Who you are *now* is not the same as who you will be at the end of this workshop," the man says. "Instead of the ordinary, 'Hi, my name is Blah blah, and I'm from Blah blah,' we're going to get to know one another through a writing exercise."

The teacher opens his laptop and flicks on the overhead. He dons a pair of reading glasses. "Use your phone, tablet, laptop or whatever electronic gizmo you have with you. Find this web site. It's called Drop In." He stops and peers at us above his glasses. "We're doing Poetry in the Twenty-first century."

He waits for everyone to find the page and demonstrates what he expects the class to do. "In this box you will type the class number, #4567, and under *Name*, write your name." He types *Dean Saunders*. "Occasionally, we will do Drop Ins anonymously, but today I want everyone to use his or her full name."

He types the words, *Some poems.* "I want you to write a line of poetry beginning with this phrase." Saunders types as he continues to talk. "Once I'm happy with what I've written, I click send, and presto." He looks up. "My masterpiece appears on the screen."

His line reads: *Some poems stand at the door shouting obscenities. Dean Saunders.*

The teacher backs away from his laptop, removes his glasses, and gestures toward the screen. "Your task is to create at least two lines beginning with 'some poems.' Keep adding lines as you think of them until I yell stop. Don't censor yourself. Feel free to get weird."

Fingers on keyboards clatter like rain against glass. I type *Some poems are like waking up in a foreign city. Michael G. Flynn.* After I click *Send*, I glance at the screen to make sure it posted.

"Don't stop and read," the teacher says. "Keep going."

Some poems conjure imaginary friends and contain silences. Michael G. Flynn

Some poems work best at night, under the sheets, when the windows rattle like freight trains and reek of Jack Kerouac's cigarettes. Michael G. Flynn

Some poems leave cigatette burns on the sheets. Michael G. Flynn

Some poems are a freeway of words, changing lanes, tailgating. Michael G. Flynn

"Okay stop!" the teacher says. "Let's take a look at these bad boys."

I scan all the lines, relieved to see I'm not the only one who made typos.

"What do you notice about them?" The professor says.

Shoe, seated next to me, says, "they're odd."

"Yes," Saunders says. "Your name?"

"Brad Xu, but you can call me Shoe."

The poet clasps his chin in his hand and looks over Shoe's lines. On the whiteboard he places a star next to

Some poems take long naps in the afternoon and saunter in past midnight. "What else?"

"Some people took liberties with how they started the lines." A girl says.

He nods. "Your name?"

"Dharma O'Leary."

He regards her lines. "I'm curious about how poems can increase *your* penis size, but I will mark this line. *This poem whispered my name in Spanish and I took it to bed.* "Anything else?"

"Someone called Axe only wrote one."

"Who is Axe?"

A tall, Nordic looking guy in the back row raises his hand. He shrugs. "I'm not a poet," he says.

"None of you is a poet yet," the instructor says. "What else do we notice?"

"They get better as we go on?" I say.

He points at me. "Better how?"

"More interesting?" The guy bores into me with his steely eyes, so I add, "They get more specific?"

"Bingo," he says. "One key to good writing, be it poetry or prose, is detail. Who are you?"

"Michael G. Flynn."

He squints and studies my lines. "I'm guessing, Michael G., you're a lonely, horny smoker."

I chuckle, as do a few others. "My girlfriend smokes."

The teacher places a star next to, *Some poems leave cigatette burns on the sheets.* "And I'm guessing Gina does not change the spelling of her surname every few minutes," he says.

A petite girl with curly dark hair giggles. She's one of the two runners from last night. The professor chooses her line *Poems are like a cat scratching at the only closed door in the house.*

"Why do you think I starred these particular lines?" the guy asks.

A guy named Shane says, "Each line almost tells a story?"

The teacher nods. "These lines invited us in." He uses a pointer to focus on a line. "I'm curious about Dion's old friends, why Brad Xu's poems sauntered in so late, and *what* Dharma's poems whisper to her in Spanish."

He sets his pointer in the tray. "My name is Dean Saunders," he says. "I live here in Seattle with my wife, two teenagers, and a pair of the laziest dogs in the universe." He gestures to the front row. "Starting with Shoe, tell us your name, where you live, and your plans for college."

The other members of the class are from divergent places. I already know Shoe lives in Maine. Dharma says she comes from India. She seems pale for an Indian, but she wears a tunic and scarf.

The only other person from Ohio is Gina, who's from Cleveland.

"Some of you have already decided you are not poets," Saunders says. He leers at Axe, who comes from Boston. Axe smirks. "And some of you may never be working as poets, which is unfortunate because there's so much money in it."

I stifle a laugh, and Dean continues. "All writers are poets on some level, yet not all writing is poetry."

That reminds me of the line from the movie *Howl* about how poetry can't be translated into prose because it is poetry.

"I can't guarantee any of you will become poets," Saunders says. "I *can* guarantee you will become better writers through studying the craft of poetry."

Walking to the dining hall after class for lunch, Shoe says to Axe, "You pissed off the teacher on the first day."

Axe shrugs it off. "Like I said, I'm not a poet."

"Neither am I," I say, "but, it makes sense for us to study it."

"Poetry's for suicides and sissies," Axe says. "I'm only in it because creative nonfiction was full."

"How did you get the name Axe?"

"It's my initials," he says. "Alan Xavier Ellis. I think Axe fits me better."

Ass is more like it.

***

Later, after dinner, Hunter, Axe, and a couple other guys congregate in our room for study hall. I stay a few minutes, but the room feels claustrophobic.

"I've got some *actual* studying to do." I grab my bag and they all razz me about being a teacher's pet. I flip them the bird and leave.

At Drumheller Fountain, I sit on a bench, and open the notebook from poetry class. I scan the three poems Saunders asked us to read and analyze. The whoosh of the fountain provides a tranquil backdrop as I underline passages, trying not to think about Shelly. A poem called "For What Binds Us" by Jane Hirschfield makes that impossible.

I slam my poetry notebook closed, wishing I'd stayed in the dorm and gotten drunk.

Chapter Twenty-Four
Shelly

At breakfast, as the ocean slaps against the shore, Shelly pulls ripe papaya from the fruit bowl, bites into it, and sucks at the juice before it dribbles down her chin. This is how she learned to kiss.

When she was eleven, she went to a slumber party where the girls watched a French film. One of the characters instructed the other on the art of kissing by using fruit. "Take his lips against yours as if he's a juicy peach and you want to devour him."

Michael kisses like that. She wonders if he saw the same film.

Paradise is blue and clean, and it's like living inside a postcard, yet she feels empty.

Shelly doesn't understand why it feels like someone took wire cutters to the fence holding her together, snapping one link at a time.

Later, she and Josh trek toward the beach. They drop their towels on the sand and race toward the waves. Unlike the pool's still waters, the ocean makes Shelly fight to stay upright, as if it's a monster that may devour her if she's not paying attention.

As the surf spills over them, Josh says, "I still don't get why you split up with a guy who you clearly care a great deal about."

"It's for his own good."

"But why punish yourself?"

Shelly submits to a wave and pops up fully soaked. "Michael deserves better."

Josh shakes his head and swims away. "Women. You were put on this earth to confuse men."

After an hour of pushing against the surf, Shelly and her brother change clothes and find lounge chairs on a shaded lanai. They dine on cheeseburgers, fries, and iced tea as they read from the books they brought.

Josh closes his econ book. "Hey, I know what'll make you feel better. That girl I met earlier on the beach invited us to a party at her place tonight."

"Awesome."

"Maybe you'll find another damaged soul there to save."

She swats him with her book.

The sea churns a few feet away and Shelly is lulled into a dreamless nap.

Later, Shelly showers, changes into a sun dress and flip flops, and goes into the living room. Josh is snipping price tags off a couple pairs of shorts.

"Did you buy new clothes?"

"I had to. When I was packing, I couldn't find any of the new Dockers Mom bought me."

Shelly gives him a thin smile. She knows exactly where those khaki shorts are; they're on Michael's legs. Thinking of Michael sends a spike through her. Did she do the right thing by releasing him?

Once he finds his father things will be fine. They can both start over. Clean the slate. Reinvent themselves.

She imagines this new self-soft spoken, polite, much like her mom. When they get back to Ohio she'll take her mom up on the offer for the yoga class. Clear out her mind and body.

But at the moment she needs a cigarette and a drink.

"I'll be ready in a sec," Josh says. He goes to his bedroom of their suite to dress.

Shelly opens the mini fridge and pulls out a tiny bottle of white wine. She unscrews the cap and takes a swig. "I'll be on the lanai smoking a cigarette."

From the balcony, the waning sun casts a pink hue over the water, sand, and sky.

The first drag on a cigarette feels like a hand on her shoulder, a voice telling her she'll get through this moment. Followed with a slug of cheap wine, Shelly feels her body reset.

She can't imagine getting through life without chemical enhancement. Her father definitely relishes his nightly scotch. He has to deal with boring-ass law stuff all day and commute an hour each way. Even her yoga instructor mother enjoys a nightly glass of wine or two.

Aren't we all just rabid dogs at heart? Sniffing the ground for scraps?

She thinks of a line from the book she's reading where a teacher commented how the public expects teachers to be role models, yet many of the kids are "raised by wolves."

Shelly was raised by responsible, sensible people, yet she is far more feral than Michael, who *was* raised by a pack of wolves. Of the three kids in his family, only

Michael has gotten into any real trouble. Yet overall he turned out okay.

If Shelly's birth mother had kept her, would she even be alive right now? Most likely Valentine Falls would have lived in a succession of foster homes. Maybe she'd be a heroin addict or a hooker. Maybe both.

Did Shelly's mother discard her because she loved her, or because she didn't?

Shelly doesn't blame her adoptive parents for the things she's done. They've done the best they can with her. Josh turned out great. None of his DNA is tainted. Shelly's a mix of drugs, booze, and bad decisions.

Josh is right; the Millers didn't need to move to Rooster to protect her. Mayhem is in her nature. She breaks hearts all over the world. She should write an instruction manual on how heartbreak.

Her brother comes out of his room wearing new shorts and a multicolored Hawaiian shirt.

"You look like you're wearing my suitcase," she remarks.

They join their parents on the beach for a luau where they eat roasted pig and watch performances of native song and dance. Her parents allow Shelly to order another *wicked wahine*. The drink is sweet and juicy, but she can't shake off her melancholy.

Later, Shelly and Josh stride along the beach to the party Josh mentioned earlier. "She said it was a half mile this way," Josh said. They carry their sandals and walk barefoot to the girl's house, the sand still warm on their toes.

"How different would our lives be if we'd grown up here instead of Ohio?" Josh asks.

"You'd be a surf bum, no doubt."

"And you'd probably be a cult leader."

Shelly laughs. They walk toward loud, thumping music.

Josh points to a fire ring up ahead, surrounded by a group of people. "This must be it."

As they near the house, a girl with honey colored hair yells. "Josh!" She runs up and hugs him.

"Melinda, this is my sister Shelly."

Melinda grabs each of their hands. "Come on and meet everybody."

She and Josh are handed drinks. Shelly gulps hers down quickly and goes in search of another.

Halfway through her third one, Shelly joins a circle of people to dance to a Pitbull song. She yells "Fireball!" along with the others at each refrain. She sways and jumps and mimics their laughter.

How can she be with all these people yet feel so alone? Shelly refills her drink and steps away from the other dancers.

Nights are difficult. Things disappear in darkness, the way her mother did all those years ago. Chunks of memory spit out images of dark sky and snow.

Shelly is a broken glass. She can keep pouring in more wine or fire and sand, but it will never be enough. The glass will remain empty, cracked like an old piece of crystal. Whatever she adds will slip through her fingers.

Shelly gulps the rest of her drink and throws her glass, but it lands with an unsatisfying thud. The beach is too soft. She wants a hard landing, one that will bruise her.

She balls her hands into fists and punches her stomach. She feels nothing. She punches again. And again.

"Hey, are you okay?"

Shelly turns, and a guy who resembles Michael stands near. His chest is bare. She stumbles toward him. "Are you real?"

The guy chuckles. "As far as I know."

She runs her hands over his pecs. He's warm as a furnace and smooth as stone, but when she looks up, his eyes aren't Michael's.

She decides she doesn't care.

Chapter Twenty-Five

Dear Shelly,

Maybe you're in a dead zone and that's why you won't text me back, so… I thought I'd try email.

So far, my classes are good. My poetry teacher, Dean Saunders, is scary- he's a wiry guy with fierce eyes who looks like a rabid ferret. My creative nonfiction instructor, Frank Barnes is a friendly, gray-haired guy known for writing sports biographies.

My first assignment for Frank is to use an old photo of me between the ages of five and twelve. Initially I thought I was screwed because there are no photos, but then I remembered those old pictures Annie found last summer of Jeff and me when we lived in Columbus, so I texted Annie to email me a couple of the kid pix. Remember how you said I used to be cute?

Those images brought up bittersweet memories of when my good life suddenly turned to shit, so I haven't looked at them since. I'm already dreading this assignment.

We're supposed set a timer for ten minutes and write a memoir of the moment three ways: past, present, and future.

I still haven't heard from my father, so that's a lost cause. Why am I here again? Oh yeah. YOU. It's all your fault.

Since your goal is to make me suffer, you'll enjoy my laundry debacle. This afternoon I had time to wash clothes, so I gathered my dirty clothes, which is everything except what I was wearing, and carried them down to the laundry room. Well, shit. I didn't have laundry soap. I ran back upstairs (three flights!) and brought down my shampoo. Only to discover the machines don't take money--only preloaded key cards.

I hauled my crap back upstairs and washed a couple of shirts, a pair of shorts and some underwear in the men's room sink. I may as well still be living in The Whale.

I figured my roommate Hunter wouldn't care if I draped wet clothes all over the room. It's looked way worse in here. I hung the shirts in the window and slung the boxers and shorts over the back and arm rests of my desk chair.

At dinner I didn't see Hunter or any of my drinking accomplices, so I sat with Shoe (you met him at the reading) and he introduced me to more people.

"Do you know where to get a laundry card?" I asked.

"You have to buy them at the campus bookstore," he said. "Once you have one though, you can reload it at a kiosk in the library or here in the dining hall."

"Thanks." I related my tragedy of not having soap or the coin card and how my dorm room now looks like a Third World country.

He laughed. "You could have borrowed my card."

Shoe's a good guy. I like Hunter and the others, but I sense Shoe and I will become good friends.

Anyway, I have Theo's class tomorrow, so I'll let you know how things go there. No doubt more torture.

Love,

Michael.

I click Send, and then I download the three photos my sister attached in a message. I haul my backpack to the library to work on the creative nonfiction assignment. On the way I stop at the bookstore to buy the laundry card.

Inside a cubicle I study the images Annie sent.

Past: It was fall, and I was six years old, wearing jeans, brown suede shoes, and my favorite plaid shirt. My brother Jeff and I were running through leaves at Whetstone Park in Columbus close to where we lived. My mother was holding our baby sister as my stepfather, Bob, snapped photos of us. I had the unworried look of a child whose needs were met. I remember this was a time when my mother was also at her happiest as well. Bob took good care of us.

Present: I'm running toward the camera, crunching leaves under my feet. I'm wearing my favorite plaid shirt, tossing leaves in the air with my younger brother Jeff. The air smells of trees and sunlight. It's cool enough I am wearing a scarf, but not a coat or gloves. Jeff and I grab handfuls of leaves and toss them at our stepfather as he snaps our pictures. We are all laughing.

I don't look like my brother except for our matching brown and blue plaid shirts. I have brown hair and his is icy blonde like our mother's. My baby sister looks like Bob, with cocoa skin and curly black hair. But at this moment it doesn't matter that I look like nobody in the family. It's a good day to be alive and play in the leaves.

Future: The boy in the picture is joyous, but that happiness will be short lived. Maybe too much joy is a harbinger for tragedy. Shortly after this moment, the photographer, who is also the child's stepfather, will die from a fatal gunshot wound.

The boy and his siblings will face years of unhappiness, while his mother succumbs to mental illness. She will try to assuage her grief by filling her home with objects. Things accumulate—useless, broken things— and her children will not be able to breathe inside her rooms. One by one they leave her. In many ways the boy has never recovered from the gunshot that took his stepfather.

"Shit. I don't want to relive my life." I slap my laptop closed and go for a run.

Chapter Twenty-Six
Michael

Theo's fiction workshop meets Wednesday mornings and Friday afternoons. Three people from my other classes are in here: Axe, Shoe, and Dharma.

I look for clues in Theo's eyes about Shelly and what they did together those last two nights alone. His face reveals nothing.

After everyone states their names and where they're from, Theo hands out blank index cards and asks us to take one. "I want you to write an intriguing fact about yourself."

He lifts a stack of cards out of his briefcase. "For example, here are a few from a class I taught last quarter." He shuffles through the cards. "I was a singing waitress. I once shaved my cat. My family lived in Mozambique for two years. My brother wants to get gender reassignment."

He sets the cards down. "Don't write your name, only the fact. When you're finished, place the card face down on your desk and I will collect it."

I try to come up with a fact Shelly hasn't told him. He knows about my community service and living in my car. Does he know about Annie living on the back porch? Shelly probably divulged my entire life story as they lay drunk and naked together on his mattress last Friday and Saturday night.

I write, "I was conceived in the prop room of my parents' high school," and slap the card over. Just as I reach for the card to change my fact, Theo snatches it.

155

After Theo collects all the facts he shuffles them. He selects the top one and writes it on the whiteboard. *I once tried out for American Idol.* "What do we know about the story here?" he asks.

"He or she can sing," says a girl.

"Maybe," Theo says.

"Yeah, not everyone who tries out for those shows can sing," Axe says.

"He or she likes to sing, or *thinks* they can sing," Shoe adds.

Theo nods, and paces. "Okay. What else?"

A girl from the back row says, "Most likely they are young."

Theo sets the marker down on the tray in front of the board and clasps his hands. "Would this make an interesting story?"

"Sure," Dharma says.

"Why?"

"This person has a lot at stake."

"Good." Theo pulls the next card. "What makes this one interesting?" Theo writes mine on the board, and I feel myself burning from the inside out.

"Why a prop room?" the girl from the back asks. "Are they backstage during a performance?"

"Or teachers?" Axe says. "Maybe both are married to other people and they have sex at school in a secret room."

"How does he or she know about their birth origins?" someone says. "Is it some long shameful legend?"

"Or maybe the janitor caught them doing it."

A vision of Earl catching my parents pops into my head. Of all my shithouse of secrets, why did I choose that one?

"Or the kid goes to the same high school and finds out from one of the teachers, 'oh, *you're* the one conceived in the prop room.'"

"Or maybe the kid has a superpower?" Shoe says. "Like the kid sees visions of his own conception."

The class, including me, laughs. In a way I *have* watched what happened through reading my mother's diary.

"Gross!" Dharma says. She douses her palms with hand sanitizer and rubs them together.

"Okay," Theo says, "I think we get the idea of how a single event can conjure a story."

He shoots me a glance. I'll bet he knows that's *my* card, the rat bastard.

Chapter Twenty-Seven

Dear Shelly.

I think my head will detonate. I'm eating and breathing words. So far none of my classmates has jumped off the Aurora Bridge, but we all wear the physical and emotional exhaustion on our faces. Also, some of us party too much.

Before breakfast I ran three miles with a couple of girls named Gina and Andrea. I drank and toked way too much last night, though, and I stopped halfway through and threw up in the bushes. The girls found this hilarious. I flipped them the bird and dashed ahead.

Today was our first critique in Theo's class. I reworked my terrible story all morning, but even revised, it still sucks. It may be worse.

At least writing it didn't bleed me dry like what I turned in yesterday for creative nonfiction class. We were supposed to weave the past, present and future together into a single narrative, but I couldn't revisit what I'd written, so I sent Frank my draft.

In Theo's class, after each story, we discussed its strengths and weaknesses, and I recognized my own weakness by seeing mistakes made by others.

We ran out of time before it was my turn at the guillotine so I have time to screw it up more. I'm learning a lot about what's wrong with my writing. Ugh. Why didn't I go to school to become a plumber?

Theo says he hasn't heard from you either, but you're probably still alive since we haven't heard of any tsunamis or volcanoes on Maui.

***

After a craft talk given by writer Steve Almond, a group from my fiction class saunters out of the auditorium together. "He was awesome," Shoe says.

"He's full of shit," Axe says. "You don't have to slit your wrists or write fifteen drafts to get published."

"He wasn't talking about getting published," Shoe says. "He was talking about writing well."

"Whatever," Axe says.

"I like what he said about keeping your bullshit detector on alert," I add.

Shoe stashes his iPad in his bag. "Anyone want to go check out Emerald City Books? I have directions."

"Sure," I say.

Shoe, Axe, Meredith (friend of Axe's), and I take a short bus ride from the university to Wallingford where the store is located. The store carries new and used books and is connected to a restaurant with an outdoor cafe.

At the entrance my phone buzzes. It's a 206-area code. Holy shit! My voice catches as I tell the others, "I have to take this." They go inside without me.

My whole body loses air as I push 'Accept.' I find my breath, and say, "Hello?"

"Hello," a female voice says. "Is this Michael Flynn?"

"Yes." My brain clicks into overdrive. Is this my father's wife telling me he's dead? His attorney telling me to back-off-Jack?

"Good afternoon. I'm Marianne Gault from the registrar's office. We have two addresses listed for you and I wanted to verify which is your primary address."

"Oh." I'm simultaneously relieved and disappointed. "The one on route Sixty-two."

"Okay. Thank you very much."

I stare at the phone, tempted to hurl it across the parking lot. What the hell? Why hasn't he called? Oh yeah, because I'm my mother's son. Clearly not good enough.

I check my phone again, but just the time, date, and the wallpaper picture of Shelly appear on the screen. No other messages.

"Everything okay?" Shoe asks, when I join him in the store. "You look a little spooked."

"It was nothing." I stash my phone in my side pocket.

Shoe nods and pats me on the back.

On the bargain table I spot a used copy of *Kerouac: the Road Novels 1957-1960* for ten bucks. It's in good shape and includes a few notes and underlined passages. Shelly once told me she bought a book because it had a letter inside and she was more interested in the letter than the book. Should I buy it for her? She didn't say she never wanted to see me again.

Shoe and I separate and I make my way to the science section. I do a double take when I find one of my father's books. It's a paperback entitled, *The Best of Earth is Underwater*. Reviews on the back cover call it "Startling and informative," "a must read for anyone who cares about the future of the planet," and "Ashton Meadows provides a fresh perspective on looking at the world from the bottom up."

Shoe comes around the corner and notices me studying my father's book. "You're into science?"

"Somewhat." I don't feel like revealing that Dr. Meadows is my long, lost father. I'll save that saga for another day. Or never.

Blue Valentines

Chapter Twenty-Eight
Shelly

Shelly is lying on the beach when dawn light wakes her. She sits up and blinks, trying to recall how she got here. Nearby an empty bottle of Crown Royal rests on the sand.

Shelly sees Russell striding toward her holding two paper cups of coffee. "I don't know about you, but I feel like I got run over by a truck." He hands her one of the cups. "I wasn't sure how you took it so it's just black coffee."

"Thanks." She takes a drink and looks around. "Where the hell are we?"

He plops on the sand next to her. "I think we're still at the party."

Shelly shakes sand out of her hair. "The last thing I remember we were doing Jell-O shots on a balcony."

"You were shouting quotes from Jack Kerouac's *On the Road*. Then we came down here for a naked midnight swim."

Shelly looks down. She's wearing the dress she wore last night, but no underwear. Her shoes are also missing. "You've read Kerouac?"

"For Twentieth Century Lit."

"What did you think?"

He shrugs. "It was okay. Parts of it were funny."

"Do you have a favorite book?"

He looks out at the sea. "I always thought Kafka's *The Metamorphosis* was pretty original."

"Hmmm." Russell *isn't* the mental midget he seemed like last night.

She and Russell finish their coffee and creep into the house to find her sandals and his shirt. Her underwear is a lost cause. He walks her back to the hotel, where she changes clothes and joins her parents and Josh for breakfast.

Chapter Twenty-Nine
Michael

Axe is first up on the chopping block. Everyone praises his dialogue and descriptions, but Theo, who always has the final word, says, "This story is all surface. Your language is tight, the action interesting, and the dialogue is snappy, but I don't care what happens to…" Theo picks up the pages and scans them. "Harold. He could be any random handsome guy I see on some action adventure movie. He's beige, and his story is beige."

Theo sets Axe's story down. "Do you care to rebut?"

Axe grips his pen as if he's about to stab Theo with it, and I almost feel sorry for him. "Explain what you mean."

"Good fiction has both external and internal conflict." Theo stands up and draws a diagram on the board that looks like a fish with a water line through it. "There's the apparent story, what happens above the water." He draws a wavy line above the water line, and then adds several marks below the line. "And there's the *underlying* story, or what's *really* at stake.

"For example, in *The Wizard of Oz,* the *apparent* story is Dorothy wants to get back to Kansas." He marks an X on the upper curve of the fish and writes 'Kansas.' "The *underlying* story, however, is she holds the power within herself to return any time; she just doesn't know it. She has to discover it through a series of events." He writes 'unknown power within' under the water line.

He points his chalk stick at the class. "This applies to *all* of you, not just Axe."

"How do we do that?" Dharma asks.

Theo sets the chalk down. "One way is to use the best point of view for which to tell your story."

"Like if Axe had used the killer's viewpoint instead of third person?" Shoe says.

Theo rubs his chin. "Yes, taking the less obvious point of view is one way to solve it." Theo straddles his chair and faces us. "The novel *The Art of Racing in the Rain,* could have been told by Denny, the human hero's point of view. It would have been a decent story about a guy who races cars, marries, falls in love, has a child, and later, his wife gets sick.

"But Garth Stein kicks the story up several notches when he chooses to narrate it from the *dog's* perspective. Enzo the dog has an extraordinary voice, and we fall in love with him, and therefore we fall for the humans, too."

Theo stands up again. He paces and forms a steeple with his fingers. "Here's what I want you to do. Take the piece you just wrote but turn it around. If you narrated your tale in first person, redo it in third, and vice versa. Or take the antagonist's point of view." He eyes Axe. "Give random guy number one a good *reason* for slicing up random guy number two."

"When do you know when it's good enough?" someone asks.

"Sometimes you don't," Theo says. "Sometimes you need someone else to tell you whether or not it works. That's why you take a workshop like this where you get productive feedback."

"Is shredding someone's work productive?" Axe says.

"It can be," Theo says. "As a writer, you have to be willing to face tough criticism. Sure, we all want accolades, but sometimes we don't deserve them."

"Do you ever reach a point when you don't need outside input?" a guy asks.

"Yeah. When you're dead." Theo says. "That's what Steve Almond meant by finding the bullshit detector. Once you've developed confidence in your work and mastered your own bullshit detector, you become less dependent on outside evaluation. But you need to write a lot and read a lot. And fail a lot."

He gestures toward his computer sitting on the desk. "I have two failed novels stored on my laptop right now. And the next one I write will either work or it will fail less."

"How do you know they failed?" Dharma asks.

"Because I lost interest," Theo says. "If *I'm* not engaged, the reader definitely won't be. You have to believe in the story, or the work fails."

"But there's a plethora of bad writing out there that gets published." Axe says. "I mean, look at *Fifty Shades of Gray*. She's making money hand over fist."

"True," Theo says. "But is that the kind of writer you want to be?"

Axe gives a nervous laugh. "Maybe, if I can buy a yacht and my own private plane."

"Then you probably shouldn't have taken this workshop."

Axe looks like he's about to retort, but he remains silent. Theo glances at the clock. "See you Friday," he says.

I hang back and walk outside with Theo. When the others are out of earshot, I say, "You were pretty rough on Axe. I mean, he can be a douche bag, but ..."

"That arrogant son of a bitch. He writes well, but most likely he'll write the kind of chaff that makes money rather than has redeeming value." He shrugs. "I'm just not materialistic enough to sell my soul for a house with a pool and a private jet."

We walk a few paces, and he asks, "Have you heard from Val...I mean Shelly yet?"

"Not a word."

"Don't worry," he says. "Val kind of zones out when something weighs on her mind."

That makes me wonder what *is* weighing on her mind. "I wish I could find the key to her vault of secrets."

"Good luck with that."

"Did she close up when you were in San Francisco?"

He stops walking. "Yeah. Especially when we looked for her mother and couldn't find her. She'd retreat for a few days, and then we'd start searching again."

"Right before we came out here, Shelly found out that her mother is dead."

He nods. "She told me. But Val always held onto hope."

"How did she act after I moved into the dorm?" I ask. "When you guys were alone together, did she seem okay?"

Theo grins, and puts a hand on my shoulder. "Are you trying to ask me where she slept?"

"Sort of. I guess I want to know if I should hire Axe to kick your ass."

He laughs. "Your girlfriend slept in my bed, but I stayed in the recliner."

I'm not sure I believe him, but I let it go.

Chapter Thirty
Shelly

Shelly walks back and forth along the shore with her phone, her arm outstretched like the Statue of Liberty. "I found a signal!" she yells to Josh. She scans through to see a dozen texts from Michael. She punches up Facetime.

After several rings, Michael's face appears on the screen.

"Hey!" she says.

"Finally. Where the hell have you been? It's been like a week and a half."

"Hello to you, too."

"Sorry, but I thought you were sliced into pieces and fed to the sharks."

"So maudlin, Neruda."

"What was I supposed to think?"

"That I'm alive and having fun at the beach."

He doesn't respond.

"Look!" She turns and shows him her shoulder.

"Is that a bruise?"

"I got a tattoo!"

"Oh."

"It's a dolphin. Isn't he cute?"

"I guess?"

"You don't sound very convincing," she says.

"I'm just tired, that's all."

"Too much partying?"

He chuckles. "Writing my ass off. It's hard to hear you. Are you at the beach?"

"Uh-huh. Can you hear the ocean? Wanna see it?"

"Sure," he says. "Show me the ocean."

She pivots her phone toward the sea. "Can you see it?"

"Move closer."

They both listen for a couple of minutes. "It's fantastic," he says. "Hard to believe we're on the same planet."

"I know," she says. "I could live here."

"I miss you."

"Are you lonely? I thought you made some friends."

"Aren't we all lonely? I mean, we all die alone eventually."

"Geez, Neruda, you really know how to brighten up a conversation. I'm so glad I called you."

"Like you said, all my sides are dark," he says.

His negative energy is killing her buzz. and she's tempted to just hang up on him. Behind her the Pacific thrashes against the shore. "Can you imagine if Neruda or Kerouac had an iPhone?"

"Neruda would have thrown his into the ocean," Michael says. "And Kerouac would be downloading porn."

She laughs. "There's the Neruda I know."

"Speaking of Kerouac, I'm in Theo's fiction workshop," he says.

"I know. He told me. Is he a good teacher?"

Michael narrows his eyes. "What else have the two of you discussed about me?"

"Seriously Neruda? Have I asked you to explain about all the girls you go running with?"

"Oh, so you *do* read my messages."

"I'm sorry I haven't replied, but ...well, I *am* on vacation."

Michael bites his lip. "Yeah, yeah."

Shelly stumbles on the sand. "What else have you been doing?"

"Writing, reading, running, going to lectures."

"I mean for *fun*."

"That *is* fun for me."

"My God you're a wack job," she says. "How come I never noticed that before?"

"Maybe because you're wackier?"

"Ha ha."

"By the way," he says, "I bought you something."

"I love presents! What is it?" Suddenly, Russell creeps up and grabs Shelly's waist. She giggles, and drops her phone. "Russell, stop!" she squeals.

Shelly picks up her phone and blows sand off the glass. "Sorry. I'm back."

Russell pokes at her. She laughs, and pushes him away. "You may be cute but that doesn't mean I won't try to drown you."

"Who's that?" Michael asks.

"That's Russell."

"Is he someone you just met on the beach?"

"He's...I'm on the *phone*!" Russell unsnaps her bikini top. She yelps and grabs it before giving Michael a boob shot. She shoves him away again. "He's a big *dumbass* is who he is."

Shelly faces Michael again. "I told you my next boyfriend would be dumb, and *he's* dumber than a box of rocks."

"Your...*what*?" The look on Michael's face makes Shelly realize she needs to end this call now. She should have answered Michael's emails and texts instead. "Listen, I've got to go. My parents are taking us all out to dinner tonight and I have to wash the sand out of my hair."

She disconnects without saying good-bye.

I am such a monster, she thinks.

She pours herself a full glass from the rum punch Melinda brought and downs half of it in one gulp.

Chapter Thirty-One
Michael

Theo needs 2,500 words before the next class, so I don't have time to ponder the state of Shelly's and my relationship.

Axe shares a story where the protagonist dismembers his victim slowly with a saw. Before the victim dies, he suffers under excruciating pain and gratuitous violence that grosses most of the class out, yet it's well written. The narrator is creepy and seductive at the same time. I figure he pictured Theo as he wrote it.

"Thanks for the nightmares I'll have tonight," Dharma tells him. She rubs sanitizer on her pale fingers. I wish I could use some of that to wash the images out of my brain.

All Theo says is, "Dexter fans will find it compelling." I think he's already given up on Axe.

After workshop, I walk with Theo and tell him Shelly finally called, but I don't add she was with some guy. "She showed me the ocean on her phone. That was so cool. I've never even been to a real beach."

"Do you want to go to the beach?" he asks. "It's not exactly Hawaii, but there are several nice beaches around here."

"Really? How would I get there?"

"I'll borrow Dale's car and drive us up to Richmond Beach." He claps me on the back. "I think you could use a break, and the sea might knock out some of that anxiety."

We walk to his apartment and get Dale's keys.

"Do you mind if I drive?" I ask. "It's been almost two weeks, and I miss the feeling of a steering wheel in my hands."

"Sure," Theo says. "I'll navigate."

It's a familiar rush sitting behind the wheel.

Theo directs me west until we hit highway 99. Aurora Avenue is a long stretch of cars, buses, strip clubs, seedy bars, crummy motels, shopping centers, and people. "Where do all these people come from?"

"Everywhere," Theo says. "Some even come all the way from Rooster, Ohio."

I chuckle, and keep driving.

Theo guides me to Richmond Beach and I park in the lot. The coastline draws me toward it. Theo's right. The ebb and flow of water runs a hand over me as if to say, "just chill, dude."

I glance at the miles of water. "Wow. The world is large and small at the same time."

"What do you mean?"

"This ocean connects me to someone in Japan or Russia, and to Shelly in Maui, and yet it's also right here."

"We're not actually on the ocean itself," Theo says. "The nearest ocean beach is about a hundred and twenty miles."

We trek along the sand. Rocks, shells, and large branches lie on the beach. It's a warm, clear afternoon, and I feel myself decompress.

"Walk barefoot on the sand," Theo says.

I slide off my Nikes and socks. When my toes dig into the sand a primal memory seeps into my skin, back to when Jeff, Annie, and I were kids when my stepdad Bob was still alive. "This sand takes me back to before our lives turned to shit."

"That shitty life got you into this workshop."

I shake my head. "I'm here because of Shelly."

"What do you mean?"

"I didn't even know about this thing until she found it online. *She* filled out the application, hijacked my college entrance essay, and got my references." I gaze at the water. "Shelly was determined to get me to Seattle."

"Why?"

"My father's here."

"Oh, I'd like to meet him."

I shove my hands in my pockets. "So would I."

Theo gives me a bewildered look.

Shelly must not have revealed every detail of my life to him. "He doesn't know about me. I mean, not until the day I flew out."

I fill Theo in about spending my life wondering who I am and how Shelly and I uncovered the secret. "My mother doesn't even know the real reason I'm here."

"You're the one who was conceived under the stage?" Theo asks.

My face reddens and I turn toward the shore. I guess he *didn't* know about that.

"Have you connected with your father?" Theo asks.

"No." I toss a rock at the waves. "I was perfectly content to lead my pathetic little life, but then Shelly intervened."

"You can still go back home after the workshop is finished."

I kneel and place my hand against the damp sand, leaving a palm print. "The thing is, I'm not sure Rooster is my true home."

"Oh?" Theo crouches next to me.

"Have you ever gone somewhere and you immediately know you don't belong there? That you don't fit in?" He nods.

I pick up a handful of caked sand and it crumbles through my fingers. "That's kind of how I feel in Rooster. It was more than being a poor kid with a wacked out family."

We both stand, and I brush the sand off my hand on my pant leg. "I know I *can* go back. Earl and Dot will take me in, but everything's changed. *I've* changed."

Theo gives me a probing look. "In what ways?"

I shove my toes further into the gritty earth. "Right now, while I'm standing on this beach, Rooster feels like a different universe, as if I were a character in someone else's story." I hurl another stone into the sea. "I was living my life but I wasn't thriving in it. These past two weeks I've already made more friends here than I ever did back home."

"You found your tribe here," Theo nods his head. "A collection of like-minded souls."

"That's a good way of putting it. My tribe."

Theo tosses a stone. "I felt like that all through high school, too. I had to move across the country to discover myself."

I pull my feet up from the sand. "Once Shelly goes to Baltimore, I'll be an island in the middle of nowhere again. And now I know there are unexplored corners of the world."

Theo slings an arm around my shoulder. "You'd find that out whether you stayed in Rooster or not." He slips off his shoes and tosses them next to mine. "Come on, let's go for a run."

"Barefoot?"

"The sand acts as a cushion," he says.

"What if someone steals our shoes?" I'm wearing the new shoes Paul and Jeff bought me for graduation.

"Only homeless guys steal shoes, and if they do, they need them more than we do." He starts to jog. "Come on. It's a new experience to explore."

Dodging rocks, branches, and litter, we run about a mile and double-back, collapsing on the sand near our shoes. It wasn't a long distance, but we're both breathing hard. "I think my hamstrings are on fire," I say.

"You challenge your muscles differently running barefoot on sand."

I lie back and raise my legs, pointing and flexing my feet. The sand warms my back, and I grab a handful and study it. "Sand is sort of a miracle, isn't it?"

"What do you mean?" Theo lies on his side, stretching his quads.

"Here are these miniscule particles of glass, rocks, and debris, that in their larger forms would injure you if you laid on them, but in this form, it's as comforting as a blanket."

"I never gave it much thought," he says. "Science wasn't on my radar screen in school. I was always a book nerd."

I sit up and stretch my body forward to touch my toes. "What's your dissertation about?"

Theo groans. "The official title is *Kerouac, the Beat Writers, and Their Influences on Contemporary Cultural Ideology*." He rests on his stomach and props himself on his elbows. "May I speak candidly?"

"Sure."

"I've spent so much time on Kerouac and Burroughs and the rest of the Beats that I'm sick of them."

I pull my knees to my chest. "I thought Kerouac was your passion."

"He was, but I burned out on him." He looks over at me. "I've read all of Kerouac's novels, poems, and essays. Essentially what makes his work readable is the elegant syntax and creative diction, along with the occasional brilliant insight, but so much of his work is about people who lead pointless, drunken lives."

"Yeah, I thought *On the Road* was a well written journey to nowhere."

"Exactly. But don't tell our girl. That's her favorite book."

"Your secret is safe with me." I draw circles in the sand. "Was all that work wasted?"

"No." He sits up and brushes sand off his chest and thighs. "The degree will help me get a job, and I'll likely teach a class or two on Beat writers. But I'm actually looking forward to teaching a few sections of freshman comp."

"Why?"

"Teaching writing is more black and white, but literary theory spins around in an endless loop." He shrugs. "Who knows? Maybe the burn-out is just temporary."

We share a moment of quiet, just listening to seagulls *quink quink quink* at one another and the soft slap of the water as it meets the sand.

"So, you're not really pretentious?" I ask.

He throws his head back and laughs. "When I get to talking about literature, I guess I am. Which may be part of the problem. I don't like me when I'm pretentious."

"Yeah, you're not pretentious in class," I say. "You're pretty blunt."

"I'm better at teaching writing than lit, but I didn't discover that until I was deeply immersed in my study."

"Are other PhDs sick of their topics?"

"More than you'd imagine." He lies flat on his back again. "I have many friends who are ABD—All But Dissertation—which means they've taken the courses, written proposals and drafts, but never completed the paper or project required for that final hoop." He rests his arms over his face. "I don't want to go down that road."

"What will you do when you're finished?"

"Feel tremendous relief."

"Does that pay well?"

"Smartass." He gazes out at the water. "Until I figure it out, I'll just keep being an adjunct. Maybe write another novel, or be a Kerouac quoting bartender."

"Does Shelly know you're sick of your study?"

"Nope." He sits up. "And I feel kind of bad leading Val into my Kerouac adventure, especially after finding out she ran away from home to join me." He thrusts a rock at the sea. "When she joined me, I was already losing interest in the topic. Maybe I thought she would re-energize me, and she did for a while. Her fresh energy and youthful passion kept me afloat. That is, until our money ran out."

Theo looks over at me. "Too bad you're only nineteen," he says. "Talking about the Beats always makes me want to go for a drink."

"I have an ID that says I'm a twenty-two-year-old guy from Indiana named Michael Neruda."

He slaps me on the back. "I know of a bar in Ballard that will put a smile on your face."

"Is it a strip club?"

"Better. A tiki bar."

***

When I make it back to the dorm there's a sock tied around the doorknob. Even an ignoramus like me knows what that means. Shit. Hunter and I never discussed how we'd handle bringing dates back.

I cup my ear against the door to hear if they're in the middle of things. Muffled voices and talking. I knock and let myself in the room and hold a hand up to shield my eyes.

"Didn't you see the fucking sock?" Hunter yells, as he covers himself and the person in his bed with the sheet.

"Yeah, sorry, but I uh…I needed my laptop. I have an essay due tomorrow." I walk over to my desk, grab my computer and cord, and make a quick exit.

Inside a twenty-four-hour coffee shop, I open my notebook and scan the assignment for creative nonfiction. *Choose a singular object that sparks a memory. Recreate the memory using a child as narrator.* Frank told us, "no fancy words, just look at the scene through the eyes of a child."

The stained-glass panels on the church across the street remind me of my late stepfather, so I write:

My stepfather Bob insisted we attend church on Sundays. We walked to a massive, gray building near our house. I asked Bob what those pointy things were on the roof. "Those are spires," he said. "They point toward Heaven."

He liked for my mother, brother, baby sister, and me to sit in the middle section of church. The pews were polished to an oily gloss, and I looked up to find the spires from the inside. "Why do the windows have so many colors?" I asked.

"They're made from stained glass," he'd say, "so God can find us easier." Bob was smart, and always had patient answers to my endless questions. The sun filtered in through the windows, and I wondered if Jesus lived inside the stained glass in shards of red, blue and gold.

The pipe organ moaned and Jesus looked at me. Not anybody, else. Just me. As if his backlit eyes were urging me to stop fidgeting and pay attention.

Bob and my mother were saving to buy a house, and he worked a part-time job at a carryout on Friday and Saturday nights. But we made it to church every Sunday.

The seats were hard, and the windows were the only things holding my childish attention as I imagined the stories behind the characters inside the glass. By day, their faces were radiant, as if ready to dance.

I wondered if the stained glass people disappeared at night, the way my stepfather did last time he read us a bedtime tale from The Arabian Nights. On his way to his second job he was caught in the crossfire during a drive-by. My family never went to church again.

I close my notebook and hold my head in my hands. I don't want to relive my life.

Chapter Thirty-Two
Michael

After dinner, Reed asks Hunter and me to drive to a nearby Fred Meyer with him to buy booze. Hunter claims he has some business to attend to. "Later, dudes."

"Ha!" I shout. "I guess we know what kind of business needs tending." Hunter flips me off.

Reed dons a pair of glasses that make him look the age his ID says he is. In the car, Reed says, "Flynn, you buy the same boring ass chips and Doritos all the time."

"What else goes with beer besides Doritos and chips?"

Reed shakes his head. "Hillbillies."

There's no meanness in his tone, so I'm not offended. Instead, I feign a redneck accent. "The technical term for us folks is Hilljacks."

Reed bobs his head and laughs. "Good to know. I'm just glad you're not an Okie."

We buy several bottles of wine and I pay for a six pack of Mike's hard lemonade. "It's named after me."

Hunter, Andrea, Axe, Meredith and I assemble in Reed's room. Reed opens the first bottle of Cabernet. Reed bought real wine glasses at the store. He fills one and hands it to Meredith. The others drink beer. I try the Mike's.

Hunter and Andrea, the blonde runner with the great legs, sit on Reed's bed, Reed perches in his desk chair, and the rest of us sprawl on the floor.

"Looks like you and Flynn are the token gay couple tonight," Axe says to Reed. He slides an arm around Meredith.

"Fuck you," Reed says.

"Michael's not gay," Meredith says. "He has one girlfriend in Hawaii, and a flock of girls he goes running with."

"Look, you're making him blush," Hunter says.

"It's the lemonade," I say, a cheesy grin on my face.

"Mikey's a slut," Andrea kicks at my feet.

"I'll keep that in mind next time there's a sock on the door," I retort.

"Whoa hoa!" Axe says.

"Assholes," Reed says. "The lot of you. I don't know why I invite you to my room."

"Because nobody else likes you," Axe says.

Reed raises his glass. "To frenemies."

We all raise our glasses and bottles, and say, "Here, here."

Reed docks his phone to his Bose speaker system and Fall Out Boy thunders in the background. "My redneck friend here informs me he is not, in fact, a hillbilly. What was that term you used? A Hilljohn?"

"Hill*jack*."

Reed nods. "Is that a step above or below trailer trash?"

I grin. "Both."

"Is your town famous for anything?" Andrea asks.

"We're close to where Zane Grey was born."

"The Western writer," she says. "Have you read any of his work?"

"No," I say. "Cowboys were never my thing." I glance at Reed. "No offense, Texas."

Reed chuffs a laugh. "None taken, hilljack."

"What *do* you read?" Meredith asks.

"I don't know," I say, rattled by the focus on me. "A little of everything."

"Loverboy here reads Neruda," Hunter says. "That's the name on his fake ID."

"What's wrong with that?" Andrea says. "I love Pablo Neruda. We're reading him in my Poetry class."

"So are we," I say.

"Have you memorized any of his work?" she asks.

I deepen my voice, and say, "I want to do with you what spring does with the cherry trees."

Andrea feigns fanning herself.

"Flynn wants to do to *her* what Hunter does to her in their dorm room," Axe says.

Hunter glowers at me. "Not fair, man. Quoting Neruda in the presence of women."

I shrug. "Hey, it's how I got my girlfriend."

"I think *I'm* in love with Flynn now, too," Axe says. He reaches for me and makes kissing noises.

"People, please," Reed says. "This is a civilized party."

"No, it's not." Axe knocks me flat to the floor. I grip my beer bottle to keep it upright. "Say something to me in Neruda."

I haven't wrestled with a guy since Jeff and I were kids. I shove him off and take a swig of *Mike's*. "Your breath emits the flavor of werewolf blood. And your anus exhales the stink of cheese farts. Your fingers bear the calluses of one who walks on fire, and your eyes are like empty holes."

"Man." Axe shakes his head. "Even when you're goofing around it sounds good."

"It's all in the verbs," Reed says. He snaps his fingers. "That gives me an idea. Let's play a game. I'll say a verb and call on someone to use it in a sentence. Then that person assigns someone else a verb." He considers for a moment. "Axe, use the verb declaim."

"I got in a wreck and filed de claim."

We all laugh, but Reed shakes his head. "Nope. Try again."

"I declaim all of you are assholes," Axe shouts.

"That's more like it," Reed says. "Now choose someone."

Axe looks around. "Meredith, use the word fondle."

"I tried to fondle Axe's balls, but I couldn't find them." She grins, and pulls out her phone to look up verbs. "Andrea, use the verb reveal."

Andrea thinks for a second. "In creative nonfiction, we are asked to reveal things about ourselves we don't necessarily want others to know." So, I'm not the only one uncomfortable in that class. Andrea reaches for Meredith's phone, and scans the verb list. "Reed, use the verb initiate."

"I tried to initiate a conversation with Hunter yesterday, but instead instigated a riot of verbal abuse."

"Oooh, two verbs," Axe says. "Bonus points."

Reed looks at me. "Flynn, use the verb shroud."

I drain my bottle, squelch a burp, and clear my throat. "I want to shroud her senses with my skin and grasp her words on my lips."

"Okay Flynn," Hunter says. "All this sex talk is making me horny." He pulls off a sock and flings it at me. "Go hang this on our doorknob and get lost for a couple of hours."

The others laugh, but being part of a group is still new, so I'm not sure if their banter is friendly, or if I'm the butt of some inside joke.

Andrea elbows Hunter, and says, "Hunter, don't be such an ass."

"He can't help it," Axe says. "It's his calling card."

"Oh, like you're *not* an asshole?" Hunter says to Axe.

Reed hands me another beer. "Nice work, Flynn. Your turn to call on someone."

Meredith hands me her phone, and I skim the list of verbs. "Reed, use the verb bolster."

"Bolster. Hmmm." He taps a couple of fingers on the side of his head. "In order to bolster his confidence, Hunter tried using words with more than one syllable."

Everyone, including Hunter, laughs.

"New rules," Reed says. "Create sentences using only one syllable words so Hunter can understand them." He looks around the room and calls on Meredith.

"I like to eat oats at dawn," she says. "Flynn."

"I shoot darts at dusk with Shoe."

"Hey, how come we didn't invite Shoe tonight?" Meredith says.

187

"I didn't see him today," Reed says. "Anyone have his number?"

"I do," I say. "I can text him."

"First, let's decide if we're going to hang around here, or go somewhere else." Hunter says.

"Oh shit," Andrea slaps her thighs. "We're missing open mic. Is anyone else signed up to read tonight?"

I stand. "I am."

Reed sets his glass down. "So am I."

"Me, too," Axe says.

Reed glances at his watch. "Drink up, assholes. We have five minutes to get there."

I guzzle the rest of my beer and this time emit a giant belch that cracks everyone up. We scatter to grab our notes and meet in the hallway.

"What are you going to read?" Andrea asks me, as we all trot down the steps.

"I'm not sure yet."

"Read that story about the homeless guy," Axe says. "It wasn't half bad."

A compliment from Axe. Rare. "I don't know. It needs some work."

The auditorium is abuzz with students and instructors. Theo is seated next to the blonde poetry teacher. He sees me and we nod at one another.

Readers are assigned the front row. I sit between Reed and Axe, who both appear relaxed. I wish I'd drunk a third beer. Is this why so many writers drink? To anaesthetize themselves before they slice open their souls in public?

Reed opens his folder and sifts through some of his work. He leans to me. "I'm prioritizing. I have my top three choices ready so I don't waste time at the podium."

The pieces in the front of my folder are both memoir essays from creative nonfiction. I'm not brave enough to read about myself. I shuffle those to the back. My poems all suck, so those get stashed to the rear as well. My only option is the one I'm turning in for fiction tomorrow. It's still raw, and I know it needs work, but there's nothing left in the folder. Shit. Whatever I read will suck.

Axe is one of the first readers. "My name is Axe, and I'd like to dedicate this story to my fiction instructor, Theo Garibaldi." He reads the story where he chops up his victim, which draws a mixed reaction. A poet reads after him and resuscitates the audience with her nature poems.

Then I hear my name.

"Imagine everyone is naked and drunk," Reed whispers. I grimace and rise.

At the microphone I clear my throat. "My name is Michael G. Flynn." Inside my head I sounds like a prepubescent nerd. "I'm going to read something I wrote for Theo Garibaldi's Fiction class. I promise no one gets dissected."

The audience's laughter relieves my anxiety, and I read my story.

Chapter Thirty-Three
Michael

This time in class Axe reads a story different from his others. It's called *The Perfect Child*. The story shows a guy who trudges his way to soccer practice after his mother drops him off. The kid hates soccer, and he's only there because it's expected of him, just as he also plays piano twice a week and takes art lessons every Saturday. If he gets a B on anything, his parents deny him TV and other privileges and force him to study.

The story moves onto the soccer field where the kid half-heartedly participates. In fact, he plays the game poorly and ends up getting hurt. Badly. At the end, he's carried off the field with a shattered leg, yet he calmly accepts the pain, and the reader wonders if the kid lets himself be injured on purpose.

"Well, done," Theo says. "*This* is what I mean about how good stories explore subterranean strata. On the surface, the boy wants to please his parents and earn their love. Yet on a deeper level, his only way out is to let himself be broken. It's a brave and cowardly act." Theo studies his copy. "The title is perfect, too, because now the boy is, in fact, no longer perfect. He's damaged."

Axe mutters a quiet "Thank you," and leaves it at that.

I wonder how much truth from Axe's life lies in the tale. Maybe Axe hides his layers behind all his assholiness.

Before he dismisses us, Theo says, "you guys have all been writing your asses off, so I'm giving you a break. No weekend homework."

The class erupts in a raucous cheer, and I realize I've been here almost two weeks. It's gone both quickly and slowly.

As we walk out, I ask Theo if we could go out for a quick drink. "I kind of need to talk."

"Sure. I could use a drink. There's a great little beer joint up the street. It's kind of a sports bar, but it's not too loud."

A waitress sets a bowl of popcorn down as we slide into a booth. We order beers and brats.

"What's on your mind?" Theo asks.

I tell him about Shelly and the precarious state of our relationship, and how she called this Russell guy her new boyfriend.

Theo listens intently, and when I finish, he says, "Val's still trying to find herself. In some ways she's as old as Methuselah, and in others, she's twelve. She's a fine person, but she's also ship-wrecked. One day she'll find her way ashore. As will you, my friend."

"It doesn't feel like it."

"You guys have no idea how young you are."

"I'm not *that* much younger than you."

"Ten years," he says. "A decade out of high school produces a different animal."

Ha! He *is* older than Shelly had said. Somebody was lying.

"You guys are still fresh off the assembly line," Theo adds. "Wait until you've had the air let out of your tires a few times and gotten a few scratches and dents."

"I was born with dents," I say. "My quarter panels are all bondo and rust."

Theo laughs. "I have to admit, you're more dented than the average nineteen-year-old." He looks me over. "I envy the scars on your soul. You're able to dig deep and tread uncomfortable places."

"Isn't that what writers do?"

"Good ones. I'm not that good of a writer, though. I'm a better writing teacher than a writer."

"Yeah, you're Axe's favorite teacher."

"Axe." Theo shakes his head. "Him I pity. Prep school education, cushy home life, cushy future. Did you know his father is one of Fortune 500's richest this year?"

"He got here because of money?"

"I think his father's company subsidizes this program. What frustrates me about Axe is he has the capacity to write well. Like that story he read today. It had depth." Theo shrugs. "He'll get by writing drivel, so I can't feel too bad for him. Who am I to say that's wrong? I write the kind of books that nobody reads."

"Maybe I should stick to poetry," I say. "Professor Saunders says there's a ton of money in it."

Theo cracks up laughing. The waitress brings our brats and Theo orders two more beers.

"Am I putting you in a bad position?" I ask.

"What do you mean?"

"Aren't there rules against fraternizing with students?"

He wrinkles his brow. "It's not like we're lovers. You are definitely not my type. No tits."

I make a sour lemon face. "You're not my type either. No ass."

Theo chuckles. "If we were in a traditional campus setting, our drinking together might be a problem, but writing workshops operate under different umbrellas."

After the waitress delivers the second round, Theo leans in and says, "Val pretty much told you she wants you to move on. Apparently, *she* has. If you meet anyone here and need to be alone, just say the word. You're welcome to use my place."

"Thanks, I'll keep that in mind."

Theo finishes his brat and wipes his mouth with a napkin. He extends his arms, flexes his fingers, and cracks his knuckles. "Love is complicated whether you're in the same city or a continent apart. All the great poems and stories are about the tenuous quality of love."

"So, I'm screwed."

Theo raises his beer glass. "Most likely. Just let it happen and write a heartbreaking tale of loss in the aftermath." He downs his beer quickly and signals for two more. "What's your third genre?"

"Creative nonfiction," I say. "But I'm having trouble there."

"Why?"

"Because we need to tell the truth."

Theo grabs a handful of popcorn. "What kind of truth?"

"Memoir. I don't want to keep looking at my past. My childhood, for the most part, was atrocious."

The waitress brings two more beers. Theo takes a gulp from one and sets the glass down. "I might be a better writer if my parents had beaten me or locked me in a basement, but my upbringing was beige. Two parent home, a brother and sister. Attended Catholic church, played football and basketball. That's *my* life."

Theo drinks his glass dry. "I think I rebelled from my excruciating tedium by studying the biggest literary rebels of the Twentieth Century. But you!" He tilts his beer in my direction. "You've had nineteen years of real endurance."

"My mom never beat me or locked me in a room."

"But she messed with your head in other ways. How does a nineteen-year-old write a story like *Edgy with a Sense of Hope,* without having a macabre childhood?"

"You *liked* that one?"

"Damn right I did." He drains half of his second glass and signals for two more. His voice deepens. "The title is pretentious as hell, but the story." He shakes his head. "Only someone who has suffered great loss and anguish at your age can write a story like that."

"I don't think of my life as suffering. Bizarre, maybe, but I manage."

"You don't just manage," Theo tosses a hand in the air. "You transcend." He taps the table. "Valentine may have gotten you here, but you're holding your own. You're the real deal."

I finish my first beer as the waitress sets two new glasses down. "Keep them coming," Theo says, and he gulps the rest of his beer down and reaches for a fresh one.

"I've never had to overcome a damn thing," Theo says. "No neuroses or diseases or poverty. I mean, look at me.

I'm almost *too* good-looking. I never went through an awkward phase or wore braces or had zits." He runs his hand through his thick hair. "The worst I've suffered is a few minor heartbreaks."

"If you keep knocking back the brew, you might have to overcome alcoholism," I say.

Theo grips his beer with both hands, and I momentarily wonder if he'll fling the rest at me. But he rocks back and emits a belly laugh. "You and Val," he sputters. "You two have your bullshit meters on overdrive."

I lean closer to Theo. "I just can't feel sorry for a guy who's had it too easy."

"And you shouldn't," he says, his voice rising. "But here's the deal." He squares his gaze on me. "I got dumped today."

"By the blonde poet?"

He nods and holds his glass to his lips. "She's the reason I'm drinking tonight." He takes a big gulp and sets his glass down. "And I'm going to sit here with my ex-girlfriend's latest possibly ex-boyfriend and get shit-faced. And I'm going to need you to walk me back to my apartment so I don't get arrested for being drunk and disorderly."

"Wouldn't you rather get arrested?" I ask. "It would be an experience to write about."

"Ha! You sound like Dale." He downs the rest of his beer and points his empty glass at me. "But you *have* been arrested," he says too loudly.

"It's not something I boast about."

"But it gives you depth. "I've done very little that could be called interesting. And you wanna know why?" His words are starting to mash together. "Because you are looking at a big fraidy cat. I would rather *read* about crazy guys like Kerouac and Cassady than be one." He pounds his chest. "Because deep, deep, deep inside, *I'm* the cowardly Lion."

Theo stands and wobbles. "I need to piss." He stumbles toward the men's room. On the way, he flirts with the waitress. When she brings our next set of beers she's not quite so friendly.

Theo changes his order to whiskey, and after a couple of shots, he mutters about not having any business teaching writing, that he's the kind of phony Holden Caulfield despises. Then he says something that makes me want to hit him.

"I didn't sleep with Valentine both those nights."

"*Both*? Does that mean you slept with her *one* of them?" I grip my glass, ready to bash him with it.

Theo's eyes are slits. "She wanted to," he slurs. "But I just couldn't do that to you."

This doesn't comfort me.

Theo is too drunk to say any more, or even to walk on his own, so, after I dig for his credit card and pay the bill, I stumble-walk him home. Along the way, Theo loudly sings a U2 tune in falsetto, mumbles lines from *On the Road*, and says, "I'm going to be freaking *thirty* in a week and I've done *nothing* with my life."

Getting Theo up the steps is a challenge. Halfway up, he passes out, and Theo outweighs me by forty pounds.

I'm tempted to leave him in the stairwell because I'm unclear about what happened between him and Shelly. But twice he's told me nothing happened. So, I decide not to leave him lying there, drunk and defenseless. I knock on the apartment across the hall, and the two guys who live there help me carry Theo inside. We dump him in a recliner. I set Theo's briefcase on the floor and close the door behind me.

It's around nine when I get back to my room. I'm relieved there's no sock on the door knob. The whole dorm is eerily quiet.

Too early to go to bed, but too late to call anyone in Ohio, I check my email. Nothing from Shelly. Nothing from my father.

Yet coming here has not been wasted. It's still possible I'm the worst writer in the program, but I'm having a good time. Maybe my *apparent* life story is the search for my father, but it turns out my *underlying* tale is to find my tribe.

I reread my story *Edgy with a Sense of Hope*. It's a thinly veiled autobiography of a homeless guy who lives in an abandoned house trying to survive a cold, winter night. Not much happens, and the story ends with the narrator saying, "Like infinity, where the snow globe figures hold another snow globe, or the picture is a picture of a person holding the same picture, on and on."

The story is total crap. Maybe Theo doesn't know anything at all.

I venture down the hall to see if anyone is hanging out in Reed's room, but the whole floor echoes like an abandoned warehouse. Then it hits me: I missed the Beethoven concert.

With everyone gone I can get some work done. I try reading an essay from the text, but Theo's words repeat like a refrain, "I didn't sleep with her both those nights...she wanted to..."

I call Shelly. After three rings it goes to voice mail. Dammit. I punch the hang-up button and text.

-Shel. Call me. It's important.

The beer fridge is empty. Shit. This is just not my night. I grab my wallet and head out to buy beer. On the way, I stop to take a whizz. As I descend the stairs, raucous laughter erupts from below.

Hunter looks up. "Hey, man, where ya been?."

The truth won't do Theo any favors, so I reply, "Sightseeing."

Chapter Thirty- Four
Michael

As I wake, my phone buzzes with a text from Theo.

Thanks for seeing me home. Feeling some pain now.
☹

I laugh, and text back.

-Good. Write about it.

-Prick. Giving you the cyber finger.

After I'm fully awake, I roll out of bed and dress for a run. These drug and alcohol fueled nights are killing me slowly.

After breakfast, Shoe and I take the bus downtown to explore the city. Neither of us has much money, so we just amble around.

Every few feet we encounter scraggly people carrying ragged bundles, dragging wheeled suitcases, or sleeping in tents on the sidewalk. One guy, stinking like the inside of my mother's house, locks eyes with me and I recoil.

We sidestep the vagrants in Pioneer Square and head to Pike Place Market. I show him Left Bank Books, and we go in and browse. From inside a used paperback, Shoe finds a bookmark from another bookstore called Third Place Books. "Listen to this." He quotes from the bookmark. "To lead a rewarding life, each of us needs three places. First is the home. Second is the workplace or school. Beyond it lies the place where people from all walks of life and all social levels interact, experiencing their commonality as well as their diversity."

He slips the bookmark back inside the book. "Being a poet and writer is my third place."

I nod. "Same here. Why do we write?"

Shoe replaces the book and pulls a thick novel from the shelf. "For me, there aren't many Asian kids in Picnic Pines, Maine." He hesitates, studies me. "Gay kids are also rare. So, it's easier for me to live inside my head."

I nod, pleased that Shoe feels comfortable enough to share this detail with me. "Gay kids are rare in Rooster, too. We have them, but it's safer to stay buried in the closet."

He gives me a reassuring tap on the arm. "Don't worry about me making a pass at you, dude. My gaydar tells me you're not from my team."

I chuckle. "I did go to the Gay Pride parade."

He thumbs through the book and reads the back. "You're still not gay."

"That girlfriend you told me about back home? Is it a guy?"

He slides a book back on the shelf. "Yeah. He kind of broke up with me, though. He's trying to date girls."

"Can someone just decide not to be gay?"

Shoe reaches for another book. "There are many levels of sexuality, and you kind of know that you don't fit gender conformity by the time you're in elementary school. But few of us flaunt our differences at school."

"I get that," I say. "After my stepdad died and we moved back to Rooster, my siblings and I were outcasts. We were rusted cans from the bargain bin, and our labels listed inferior ingredients."

"It's hard being different."

"That's why I became a library nerd," I say. "Bullies rarely use the library, so I guess bookstores and libraries are my third place."

"Libraries are where super heroes are born."

We fist bump.

"When I first met you, I sensed you weren't like the rest of our crowd, but I figured it was the Asian thing. I've never had an Asian *or* gay friend before."

He grins. "I'm a two for one sale!"

I laugh. "Do your parents know?'

"That I'm gay or Asian?"

"Ha ha."

"Yeah," Shoe says. "When I finally came out, they just nodded, like they'd known all along and were waiting for me to say something."

"Are they cool with it?"

"They're concerned about hate crimes, but at least now I can marry and adopt kids if I choose."

"Even in Picnic Pines, Maine?"

He shrugs. "If I want to live openly, I'll probably move to a big city in a blue state."

"Yeah, same here," I say. "I mean, I'm a straight, white guy, but there's something that doesn't gel with where I live. I just haven't figured out what it is yet."

He chuckles. "You're a writer. Writers are peculiar."

We move to a new section, and I ask. "Do you write about being gay?"

"Sometimes." Shoe picks out a book and we take the stairs to the third floor. "I want to show the world I'm the same inside as everyone else. It's just my lens doesn't fit the same camera as yours."

I study an old poster on the wall for a Miles Davis biography. "I have kind of a confession to make."

"Oh?"

"You know when we saw those homeless dudes on the street?"

"How can you miss them?"

"The thing is," I say, "when I look at them, instead of feeling empathy, I feel revulsion."

"Some people feel the same way about being around gays, as if they stand too close to us they'll catch it."

"But I used to *be* homeless."

Shoe turns his gaze to me. "Wow. Really?"

"I lived in my car, not on the street. But still, I know what they go through every day, wondering when and where you'll eat, shower, and sleep. Of all people, you'd think I'd have sympathy. But I don't."

"How *do* they make you feel?"

I shrug. "Repulsed? Frightened? Angry?"

Shoe thinks on this. "People are a mirror, and we dislike qualities in them that we dislike in ourselves."

I give him a lopsided grin. "Is that why Theo and Axe can't stand each other?"

"Exactly." Shoe glances out of a small window on the third floor of the bookshop. "Why were you homeless?"

"My mother's a hoarder, and I couldn't stand living in her house any longer."

"So, you moved into your car?"

"It's pretty big. A 1982 Ford LTD station wagon."

Shoe scratches his head. "How did you manage?"

"I found different places to park every night. I worked part-time, so I always had a little money. Sometimes I'd use my mom's shower if I got desperate. But I slept in the car. The only people who knew were my mom, my brother and sister, and Shelly."

Shoe scans titles along the back wall. "Do you still live in your car in Ohio?"

"No. Our custodian caught me sleeping in it on the school grounds. I live with him and his wife now."

Shoe tilts his head and raises his eyebrows. "Your life is stranger than fiction."

"I know, right? Good thing I'm not gay."

He laughs. "Yeah. A person can only be so interesting."

We make our way downstairs. "Would you move here to Seattle?"

I shrug. "Maybe. It kind of depends on my father.

"You've never mentioned your dad before."

"That's because I haven't met him yet."

Shoe huffs a laugh. "I don't think I can take any more of your life."

"Try living it every day."

"I think I'll keep mine. It's less complicated." Shoe pays for his book, and we trek uphill toward Westlake to catch the light rail back to campus. As we wait, he asks, "okay, so what's the deal with your father?"

I fill him in on how Shelly and I discovered his identity by reading my mother's old journal. "Right before I flew out here I sent him a note with my phone number."

"Has he called you back?"

"No. I kind of think he never will now."

"How do you feel about that?"

How do I feel about never solving the gaps of my existence? Or never knowing my place in the world? I make a face. "I guess I just have to accept it."

Shoe clasps a palm on my shoulder. In his man-sized voice, he says. "Every man is the architect of his own fortune."

The train pulls up and we scramble aboard. I think about what Shoe said. Does the converse apply? Am I the architect of my *mis*fortune?

***

Tonight, we attend the opera. At the theater I sit next to Dharma.

"This is my favorite opera," she says. "It's so tragic and uplifting."

"Where do you go to the opera in India?"

She gives me a confused look. "India? I live in Indiana."

"Oh," I shrug. "I haven't been there either, so that's equally exotic."

"Trust me, there's nothing exotic about Indiana." She gives me a furrowed gaze. "What made you think I'm from India?"

"Your name, your long braid, and how you always wear ornate scarves and beaded tops."

She glances down at the purple and blue beaded tunic she's wearing over jeans and gives me a shy grin. "Tunics make me look thinner."

Dharma is more full-figured than Shelly, but I wouldn't call her fat. "You always look nice."

"Thank you."

The opera is in Italian, but soon, I'm fully engaged. The story is about a young geisha named Butterfly who falls in love with an American Naval officer. He eventually leaves her, which causes her heartbreak, but she holds onto the belief he will return.

He does, but by then she is penniless, and has borne his child, and the American has a wife. Realizing the officer will never reciprocate her passion, Butterfly gives his wife their child and takes her father's dagger and kills herself.

Maybe it's fatigue or sitting inside the darkened theatre next to Dharma and her musky aroma. I don't understand a word they're singing onstage, but the raw emotion from the singers' voices batters me. Dharma reaches for my hand. She and I squeeze our fingers together at the climax when the officer wails Butterfly's name.

On the bus ride back to campus it occurs to me that *Madame Butterfly* has similar elements to my mother's life. The chief difference is my mother is suffocating herself slowly with things rather than stabbing herself to death.

Chapter Thirty-Five
Michael

Theo stops me as I'm walking out of poetry class and asks if want to go for a beer.

"Just one?"

He smirks and slaps me on the back. "I promise, no drunken rants."

We go to the same bar as last Friday, and I buy Theo's beer. "Happy Birthday, old man." We clink glasses.

"Thirty." Theo sighs. "The end of my youth."

"Maybe I should have bought you a cane."

"Prick."

I chuckle. "What's on your mind?"

Theo rests his elbows on the table. "It's probably nothing, but last night I got a drunk text from Val." He pulls out his phone and shows me.

-Maybe if I walk far enough into this ocean I'll find where my mother went and discover if she has room for me.

My chest clenches. "Have you heard from her since?

"I called her this morning and she laughed it off. Said she and some friends were on the beach doing shots." He stashes his phone back in his pocket. "That girl worries me, though."

Why did she text Theo and not me? Last night I was at the opera, but checked my phone as soon as we came out of the theater. No messages.

"I'll text her and see what's up," I say. "Not that she ever replies." I pick up my glass. "Am I your date again tonight?"

"Nope." Theo raises his glass. "Just one beer. Then I have an *actual* date."

"Someone new?"

"A semi-reconciliation with Flora."

"Congratulations."

I text Shelly as soon as I leave the bar. Naturally, she doesn't respond. I stash the phone back in my pocket. At dinner I sit with a new group of people since Hunter, Shoe, and the rest of my friends are nowhere in sight. Dharma introduces me to people from her dorm, and they seem like decent people, but the text Shelly sent Theo keeps whirling through my head.

After a much-needed run, I shower, change, and throw a load of clothes in the washer. As I climb up the steps back to my room my phone buzzes. It's Shelly.

-Meet me at the airport tomorrow around 3:30. I'm flying separately from my parents because I need to talk to you.

-About what?

Naturally, she doesn't respond.

Chapter Thirty-Six
Michael

After poetry class, I grab a sandwich from the cafeteria and stop at my room to change clothes before heading to the light rail station. I wear my Jim Morrison shirt, Shelly's favorite. My hair is shaggier than when she last saw me, and I keep my five o'clock shadow. I splash on some of Hunter's Versace Eros as a final touch. She'll find me irresistible.

Still, her sudden need to see me worries me. And then there's the message she sent to Theo.

At one of the rail stops I notice a billboard. A couple is about to kiss. In red letters above the picture it says, *Love Carefully*. I decide to interpret that as a good omen.

It's a few minutes past three when I arrive. I wander around the baggage carrousels. At 3:20 Shelly texts.

-Meet me in the Starbucks in Baggage area near the N gates.

When I get to Starbucks I don't see her, even though a familiar voice calls my name. Then I spot a girl wearing a green tank top, shorts, and flip flops with a purple pixie haircut waving at me.

"Shelly?" I walk to her. "What did you do to your hair?"

She jumps up and gives me a quick hug. "I'm surprised you noticed."

"It's a little hard to miss."

"Like it?" She turns her head to and fro and shows me the back of her neck with crisscrosses shaved into it.

"It's… interesting," I say. "Your eyes look really blue."

"The beach made a mess of my hair. The black turned all brassy and felt like straw and I met this woman on the beach with purple hair and I said how much I liked it and she offered to do mine the same color for free."

I slide onto a seat facing her. This isn't the Shelly I know. This one not only looks different, she's chattering ninety miles an hour.

"Anyway, she said it would fix the brassiness, which it did, but then my hair felt like *burnt* straw, and started breaking off, so my mom took me a salon." She pauses for a breath. "It was just easier to cut it all off than to fix it."

She takes my hand and places it on her head. "Feel it."

I finger through the short layers. "It's soft."

She shrugs. "It was time for a change anyway." She takes a sip of her drink and I wonder if something in her coffee is making her so jittery.

"It's different," I say. "Is this why you wanted to meet? To show me your hair?"

She gives me a sheepish grin and flutters her hands. "I wanted to see you. And here you are, looking all Bohemian and writer-like."

"Yeah." I rub my gritty chin. "I need to look the age my ID says I am."

Something feels off, and it's not just Shelly's haircut. There's an unfamiliar tension between us, as if we're on a first date, yet our first date wasn't this awkward.

"I'm going to get some coffee," I say. "You need a refill?" She shakes her purple head.

When I sit back down, she says, "Besides the opera, what other interesting things have you done?"

"Oh, so you *do* read my texts. You just don't respond to them."

"Our signal was erratic."

I flip open the plastic tab on my cup. "Theo took me to the beach and a couple of bars."

"Hmm." She sips her coffee. I expected more of a reaction. At least a question about partying with Theo. "What else do you do for fun?" She crosses her legs. The top leg flaps like a fan blade.

"Like what?"

"Have you made any friends?" Flap flap flap of the leg.

"Yeah. Tons. I'm like part of a crowd now." I tell her about Hunter, Axe, Shoe, and the others.

"You have a friend named Shoe?"

"His last name is spelled X-U, but he pronounces it like shoe."

She nods. "It figures the shoe Nazi would hang around someone named Shoe."

"Ha ha." I reach down and stop her leg. "And I have a couple of running buddies."

She lets her flip flops drop to the floor and sits cross-legged on her chair. "You just like that runner's high."

"You like breathing nicotine, I like breathing air."

She glides a finger around the lid of her drink. "Have you met any girls?"

"Just the ones I run with."

The clichéd elephant stands in the room, swinging his trunk between Shelly and me. Our silence is filled by the whoosh of the barista steaming milk. I tinker with the lid on my cup. "Theo showed me the text you sent him."

"Which one?"

"Which *one*? How many texts have you been sending him?"

"Don't get all maudlin, Neruda."

"How am I supposed to act? You don't respond to any of *my* texts or emails, but you freely communicate with your *ex*-boyfriend about wanting to walk into the ocean to meet your dead mother."

She rolls her eyes. "You mean the other night?" She waves it off. "I was drunk. It didn't mean anything."

I grip my cup. "I think it did."

She takes a long breath and bobs her head. "I don't want to talk about it."

"You never do. You always go into lockdown when someone approaches your invisible boundaries."

She takes the lid off her drink and stirs it with a small wooden stick. "Tell me what you've learned so far in the workshop."

Of course, she changes the subject. I consider this for a few moments. "I'm learning that deep layers of truth can hurt you."

She avoids my eyes and drinks from her cup. "Have you heard from your father?"

Naturally, she puts the focus back to me. "No," I take a sip of my *misto*. "Either he never got the email or he read it and deleted it." I set my cup down. "It doesn't matter anymore. In a way, I'm relieved."

She narrows her eyes at me. "Neruda, the main reason you came here was to meet him."

"I can survive not knowing my father. I've lived this long without him."

"You can survive by breathing, eating, and drinking. But isn't this what you've wanted your entire life? To find out who you are?"

I shrug. "I'm discovering who I am through my writing."

"Is that enough?"

I clasp my hands around my cup. "Looks like it's going to have to be."

Silence slips between us again. Then I remember the Kerouac book. "I almost forgot the gift I got you." I dig through my pack, pull out the Emerald City Books bag, and slide it across the table.

Shelly breaks into a radiant smile. "Kerouac's Road Novels." She leans across the table and kisses me on the lips. "Thank you. This is awesome."

The clouds between us lift, and for a second, I believe things between us are back to normal.

The moment doesn't last.

Her voice gets shaky. "I have to tell you something."

My body tenses up. "Oh?" I swish my cup and take another drink. "I thought you said you were on the pill."

"It's not that." She casts her eyes down. "You remember that last night we spent together at Theo's?"

"The last time we made love," I say. "Duh. A guy doesn't forget a night like that."

She avoids my eyes, stirs her drink over and over. "Right. Well, I took a picture of you before you woke up in the morning."

"What kind of picture?"

Shelly stops stirring and looks up at me with her big blue eyes. "Don't freak out." She pulls out her phone and scrolls through her photos. "It's actually very artistic."

She hands me her phone, and there I am, lying on my back, sprawled on Theo's striped sheets, an arm draped over one eye, buck naked. I shrug, and hand the phone back. "So? What's the big deal?"

She stashes it in her purse and rests her hands around her cup. "You might have a problem."

I snicker. "Why? You didn't text it to my *mother,* did you?"

She averts her gaze and swizzles the stick again in her coffee. I sense there's no joke here. "It may have been posted on twitter and Instagram."

"Why would you do that?"

"It wasn't me." She hesitates and stops stirring. "Do you remember that guy Russell?"

"From the beach. Your *new* boyfriend, as you put it."

"Him, yes. Well, he and I...we..."

A flame flickers in my chest. "I get the picture. Don't need to hear your play by play with another guy." I drum my fingers on the table. "What does he have to do with a naked picture of me?"

"Well, he was going through my phone, and he saw it."

"Why was this Russell character going through your phone?"

She takes a leisurely sip from her drink and licks her lips. "I took a similar one of him, except he was still awake, and he grabbed my phone to delete it."

It takes a moment for me to process what she said. My voice rises. "So how the *hell* did *my* picture end up on the Internet?" The couple at the next table glances our way.

Shelly lowers her voice. "He emailed the photo to himself and told me he was posting it."

"Why?"

"He was jealous."

I slam my hand on the table. Both of our cups sway. "How could you let that happen?"

"I don't know." She cowers in her chair and her eyes are wet. "We were drunk, and we started fighting about shit. He didn't like that I had pictures of you and Theo."

"*Theo*?" A bomb detonates inside me.

Her voice drops to almost a whisper, and she says, "I have one of Theo, too."

"Show me."

She hesitates and pulls her phone out again. She finds the photo and I recognize the mattress on the floor, and Theo, lying on his side on the same striped sheet, exposing his well-endowed manhood.

Her voice quivers. "Russell said he posted this as well."

I thrust her phone back at her and it clatters face down to the floor. I spring out of my chair and flail my arms. "What the fuck!"

She leans down to pick up her phone. The glass is shattered.

I'm frightened of the rage inside me. Rage at Theo, rage at this Russell guy, and most of all, rage at Shelly. I want to shove my fist through all their faces, and I'm not sure who I want to hit the hardest.

I stalk back and forth and kick the side of a trash can. One of the baristas looks up, and says, "hey, man."

My hands are knotted in fists and I don't care that people are staring at me. Shelly walks toward me. "Theo, please…" Her hand shoots up to her mouth, but she can't take the words back.

I stab a finger into my chest. "*My* name is *Michael*!" I grab my bag and thrash my way to the exit.

Shelly follows, but I turn, and say, "You've done *nothing* but screw up my life since I met you. You meddle and manipulate and do things behind my back. I didn't even *want* to come here." I wave at the damaged phone in her hand. "And now *this*? It's…you… you do all this impulsive *shit* and you never consider the people you hurt." I back away from her. "Just stay away from me. Stay the *hell* out of my life."

Chapter Thirty-Seven
Shelly

As Michael backs away from her, ravaged and angry, Shelly feels the spool of thread holding her together unravel.

She rakes her fingers through her short hair. The people nearby stare at her. She shoves her toes into her flip flops, grabs her bag, and high tails it out of Starbucks.

What have I done?

She's seen Michael angry before, but never at her.

Isn't this what she wanted? For him to finally see her as the truly terrible person she is?

Shelly plunks into a chair at a random gate and texts him on her shattered phone. She cuts her right thumb on the broken glass.

-Michael, I'm so sorry. 😞 *<3<3<3 Please forgive me.*

When he doesn't respond, Shelly gets up and walks into the chaos of the terminal. She steps into a newsstand, seeking distraction, but the magazines blur together.

A man wearing a suit and holding a briefcase says, "Miss, I think your hand is bleeding."

Shelly looks down at her ragged thumb as it speckles the floor with her blood. She digs into her purse for a wad of Starbucks napkins and stanches the wound. As she presses the paper napkins over her thumb, she feels a fragment of glass jutting from it. She gasps and rushes out to a bathroom.

She holds her right hand up and uses her left to find her tweezers. More blood gushes out as she extracts the shard. She soaps and rinses her fingers. There are no paper towels, only hand dryers. Shelly ducks into a stall and unwinds a mass of toilet paper and wraps it around her thumb. Elevating her right arm, she returns to the gift shop to purchase band-aids.

As Shelly pulls out her credit card, the cashier glances at her. "I think you need more than bandages. It looks like you need a doctor."

The toilet paper around her thumb is soaked in red. "It's okay." She deserves this injury. Shelly reaches down for two packs of tissues and swipes her credit card. "Add these to my total."

She wanders over to an empty gate and sits. She dismantles her soaked paper bandage, covers the gash with the first packet of tissues, and seals it with four band-aids.

She waits.

Once her thumb stops oozing, Shelly pecks out another text with her index finger.

-*Please believe me. I never meant to hurt you.*

This time she gets a response. It says, **this message is undeliverable**.

Chapter Thirty-Eight
Michael

The thirty minutes it takes me to return from the airport has both calmed me and deepened my distress. There's still Theo to face. I don't know if I should kill him before or after warning him about our junk being on display.

I pound on Theo's apartment door. He opens it quickly. "Hey," he whispers. "Dale's asleep." He steps into the hall and pulls the door shut behind him. "What's up?"

I punch him and he falls against the wall. "I just came to say fuck you and your lying ass."

"What are you talking about?" he says, as he stands up. He rubs his chin where my fist met his face.

"About you sleeping with Shelly."

His expression tells me he won't deny it. He can't anyway. I've seen the evidence. "I'm sorry, Michael, I didn't think..."

"Oh. It gets better, because she ended up screwing both of us, literally and figuratively."

"What do you mean?"

"She took naked pictures of us while we were sleeping, and her latest boy toy found them and posted them online."

He runs a hand through his hair. He massages his forehead with his thumb and forefinger. "So how do we handle this?"

"*We* don't do anything," I shout. "You and I are not friends or buddies. We just happened to have sex with the same crazy-assed bitch."

He sighs. "Listen, let's go have a beer and talk this out." He reaches for my shoulder, but I flinch and back away.

"I'm done with you, man." I move down the stairs.

"Michael, I'm sorry. And I'm sorry I lied to you"

"I don't want anything to do with you *or* Shelly." I stop on the staircase and turn. "Oh, and you won't have to worry about any awkward encounters with me. I'm dropping out of the workshop and going back to Ohio."

He starts down the steps. "Michael, don't."

"I didn't want to apply to this program in the first place. This was all *her* idea."

"But you belong here, Michael." He winces and runs his hand over his jawbone. "Don't let whatever issues you and I have destroy your future."

"Fuck you!"

"I'd understand if you want to change your fiction section, but don't make a rash decision."

I slam the street door in his face and tramp back to my dorm.

Of *course,* there's a sock on the doorknob. "Dammit!" I pull out my phone and ear buds and dump the bag in front of the door. I don't give a rat's ass if someone steals it. It's just my crappy writing anyway.

My body and brain need to burn off the day, and I run fast and far, long enough to listen to my entire playlist.

As I jog back to campus, I see Shoe walking alone out of the dining hall. He waves, and I slow down to talk to him. "I missed dinner, didn't I?"

He checks his watch. "You have about ten minutes."

I lean forward to catch my breath. "I don't think I could eat anyway."

"You okay?

"No."

"Anything I can do?"

"Do you want a beer?" I ask. "Unless Hunter drank it all, I think we have a few left in the fridge."

"Sure." He follows me up to my room. The sock, Hunter, and Andrea are gone, and my backpack rests on my bed. I strip off my sweaty shirt and grab a towel. Thankfully, there are still four beers. I pass one to Shoe, and crack one open for myself. He and I sit in the desk chairs.

"Did you meet your girlfriend at the airport?"

"Oh yeah." I take a long pull on my beer. "*She's* my problem." I briefly tell him about the nude picture debacle. I leave Theo out of it.

Shoe nods. "Have you checked to see if it's out there?"

I wipe my face with the towel. "I don't even know the guy's full name."

"You could text her and ask."

"I never want to talk to her again."

Shoe sets his can on the desk. "How about if *I* text her?"

"That's not a bad idea," I give him her number. A couple minutes later, Shelly sends Shoe Russell's full name, twitter name, Instagram name, and phone number. Shoe gets online, follows him, and searches the guy's feeds.

"Ask when he may have posted it."

He reads her response. "She says two days ago." He checks through Russell's accounts for the past few days. Of Russell's Instagram, he says, "Nothing here but beach pictures, and a few of him and Shelly." He scans the screen a few minutes. "Nothing on twitter, either, but I'll check if this asshole posted anything on other social media."

His phone buzzes again. "She wants to know if we found anything." Shoe and Shelly text back and forth. I finish my first beer, belch, and crack open a second.

"That would be embarrassing if your package went viral," he says.

"I don't care about that. What I *do* care about is she lied and cheated on me."

"So, are you guys kaput?"

"Yeah, I think so."

"Maybe it's time for you to bat for the other team."

I chuff a laugh. "Sorry, dude. You're still not my type."

He grins and sucks down some brew. "It's hard when you can't trust someone."

"Has this ever happened to you?"

"Not exactly," he says. "At least not the dick pix. I found out my ex was dating another guy. Before he switched to girls."

I raise my beer can to him. "Thanks for helping me out tonight." My voice is slurred, even though I've only had one and a half beers. Shoe suggests I change clothes and we go eat some pizza.

At MOD Pizza we run into Axe and a guy named Claude. As we eat, Shoe shows me a new text from Shelly.

-Please tell Michael my dad contacted Russell and threatened to sue him if he posts ANY photos he took from my phone. And that I am truly, truly sorry. Michael is the last person I want to hurt.

She includes several emojis of her crying.

Chapter Thirty-Nine
Shelly

Shelly stuffs her cracked phone in the side pocket of her bag after texting with Michael's friend Shoe. Michael will cool off.

Won't he?

Two more hours before her flight to Atlanta. She changes her blood-soaked bandage and wanders through the terminal. Images of Michael's stricken face blend in with all the passengers lugging their bags. At each gate she looks for him, knowing he isn't here. She hears, "Final boarding for flight 657 to Newark. Passengers McAvoy and Campbell please return to gate B Five."

Everything starts to spin and Shelly stops to lean against a post. She steadies herself and holds her right arm against her chest. The bleeding abates.

Shelly pops into the bathroom to fix her hair, apply mascara, and lipstick. She digs through her bag for her phony ID.

In the nearest airport bar, she orders a Manhattan. "Can you make it with *Carpano Antica*?" Shelly doesn't know what that means, but that's how her father orders his.

The bartender nods and mixes her drink. He delivers a deep amber beverage with a cherry in it. The first sip is sweet and potent. She finishes the drink quickly and orders another. A waitress passes by with a plate of

French fries. Shelly leans on the bar. "Could I get some fries, too?"

The French fries arrive just as she takes a sip from her third Manhattan. She eats a few fried potatoes and stuffs a bunch of bar napkins in her bag. After she pays her bill, she walks to the Duty-Free shop where she meanders among the displays of expensive colognes. She picks up the sampler of Bleu de Chanel and sprays it in the air. It reminds her of Michael. He often rubbed this scent on himself from magazine cologne samples. She buys him a five-ounce bottle.

She also purchases a bottle of Polo and a set of Bose headphones for him. She carries her purchases to the counter and swipes her card. It comes to more than seven hundred dollars.

Is that the price for forgiveness?

What more can she do to erase Michael's hatred toward her?

Shelly staggers in the direction of her gate. She grips the bag in her left hand and finds a seat. Even though her right thumb has stopped leaking blood, she starts to shiver. She wraps her jean jacket over her shoulders but the cold is deep into her bones. She clutches her bags against her and curls into herself in the chair. She trembles and her teeth chatter.

"Honey, are you okay?" a middle-aged woman sitting next to her asks. She places a hand on Shelly's shoulder.

"I can't….stop…shiv…er…ing. it's…so…cc..old."

"Are you alone? Can I call someone for you?"

Shelly shakes harder as she reaches for her phone. She unlocks it and presses it in the woman's free hand. "Mm… my mom."

Chapter Forty
Michael

Shoe, Axe, and Claude talk me into staying. I don't explain the whole reason why I wanted to leave, because Axe and Shoe have Theo for class. I just mention Shelly slept with someone else here in Seattle. Shoe points out there's only a few days left. "The hardest part is over, man."

"And what's there to look forward to back in Rooster, Ohio?" Axe asks. Rooster feels light years away, yet my family and Dot and Earl are all there.

But so is Shelly.

"Besides," Axe adds, "you haven't smoked all your dope yet."

I laugh. "I could use some of that tonight."

We walk back to my room, and I roll a joint. After a few hits I decide I'll just skip Fiction. Theo can fail me. He failed me already.

After the guys leave and I'm alone, thoughts of Shelly surge through my head. How stupid am I? She's been hinting for months that we're done. I guess it takes a sledge hammer to my heart to get my attention.

Fly, baby bird, fly.

This is the part where the heroine sets the hero free.

All love stories end in tragedy, right? I open a Word file. You wanted me to write about you, Shelly? Well here you go, bitch.

Naked, you collect our bodies
like trophies

For your mantle of lies,

Snapshots of your betrayal.

I'm too stoned to write. I delete what I've written and set my head on the desk.

Hunter wakes me when he comes back from the shower to dress before class. I go to Poetry, and luckily there's a guest speaker so I don't have to hand in my lack of a poem.

The rest of the week I fill every moment with reading, writing, attending readings and craft talks. The time I would have spent attending Theo's class I use to craft profiles of people with ordinary jobs for creative nonfiction. So far, I've interviewed a city bus driver, a couple of people who work at Archie McPhee, a barista at Zeitgeist, and a random Geology grad student Shoe and I met at breakfast this morning.

Since I'm skipping Fiction, Shoe kind of figured out the other guy Shelly slept with was Theo. He'd seen the three of us together at the beginning of the workshop, and he noticed Theo had a big bruise on the left side of his face. "Your secret is safe with me," he tells me. "Theo told people you transferred to a different section."

I don't ask about class, but Shoe tells me Axe's stories are now devoid of violence, and Dharma wrote a semi gruesome story told through the viewpoint of the hungry wolf in Little Red Riding Hood. "She asked me if you had a problem with her," he says. "She's worried she's the reason you changed classes."

"Dharma? Not at all. Why would she think that?" Then I remember the night of the opera, and how we held hands during the performance. "I'll talk to her," I say.

It's Friday night, which is usually reserved for raucous study hall in Reed's room, but I kind of exhausted myself with my new schedule. After dinner, I walk over to Dharma's dorm and knock on her door, but she and her roommate aren't there, so I head back to my room.

As I'm about to close my email, a message pops up from meadowsash@earth.net

All my breath escapes.

My fingers twitch over the keyboard, paralyzed, as if I'm in a horror film and the voice inside my head screams, *Don't Open the Door!*

It's Schroedinger's cat, and once I open the email the cat is either dead or alive.

I take a deep breath and click on the message.

Michael,

I apologize for taking so long to reply.

I'd like for us to meet. Elliot Bay Books has a coffee shop and I'll be there this Saturday around 12:30. I hope to see you there. Otherwise, we can make alternative arrangements.

Sincerely,

Dr. Ash Meadows

"Holy *shit*!" I spring out of my seat, knocking the chair on the floor.

My first instinct is to text Shelly, but I can't contact *her*.

I pace the floor, and look around the room, knowing full well I'm alone. But still, I need to tell someone. The one person who cares the most is the one person I can't call.

Shelly got me here. She's the main reason I'm living in this moment. I'm basically lazy and wouldn't have done this on my own.

But I've been letting her steer my ship. Time for me to take the helm and be the architect of my own fortune or disaster.

But what do I do next?

Duh, Neruda, you send a reply.

Blood thumps through my temples when I re-read my father's email.

Chill, Michael. You've got this. I take a couple of deep breaths, sit in front of my laptop, and click REPLY.

Dr. Meadows,
I will see you there.
Michael

Chapter Forty-One
Michael

After a restless sleep, I shower, dress, and head straight to breakfast. Weekends are pretty light in the dining hall, and I easily spot Dharma O'Leary, sanitizing her hands. I slide in next to her. "Mind if I use some of that?"

She gives me a shy hello and hands me the bottle. With her dark hair pulled from her face and big brown eyes she resembles Audrey Hepburn. Today she's wearing a hot pink tunic and a bright green scarf.

"Thanks." I hand back the sanitizer. "I didn't stop coming to Theo's class because of you. Or what happened between us at the opera."

She takes a few seconds to respond. "Nothing happened."

"Actually something did," I say. "We shared a special moment."

She hangs her head to one side and her long bangs hide her right eye.

"I like you, Dharma. The reason I'm not in Theo's class anymore has nothing to do with you or anyone else in there." Anyone except Theo, that is. "I just needed a change."

"Okay." She places her napkin in her lap.

I swallow some eggs. "I heard you rewrote Little Red Riding Hood from the wolf's point of view."

She raises her knife to butter her toast and gives me sly smile. "Theo wanted us to imitate someone else in the class for our last story. I thought to myself, who is the furthest from my style?"

"Axe." I stab at my eggs and shovel in another bite.

She nods. "I wrote the story as if he were telling it, teeth marks and all."

I laugh. "Sorry I missed it."

"I could e mail you a copy."

"I'd like that," I nod. "Thanks."

We are quiet for a moment. "I'm meeting my father today," I say.

"Did he fly out for a visit?"

"No, he lives here."

"I thought you were from Ohio."

"I am."

She nibbles on a piece of toast.

"Actually." I set my fork down and wipe my mouth with my napkin. "Today will be the first time I've ever met him."

"Oh. There's a story there."

I scoop some eggs onto my toast. "It's a long one, and maybe someday I'll share the whole sordid tale with you."

She looks at me with those Audrey Hepburn eyes. "I look forward to it."

We finish our meal, dispose of our trays, and walk to the exit together. "I can't believe we only have a few days left," I say. "It's gone fast, hasn't it?"

"Yes, it has," she says. "I was worried three and a half weeks of this intensive schedule would drag on, but this has been so great. I've made a lot of friends. More than I ever did in high school."

"Same here."

"I sort of dreaded coming here," she says, "but now I don't want to leave."

"Yeah," I shove my hands in my pockets. "I know what you mean."

She touches my arm. "I hope your meeting with your father goes well, Michael."

"Thanks," I say. "Me too."

It's just past eleven when I arrive at Elliot Bay Books, but I need time to chill. And once I'm back in Rooster next week it'll be an hour's drive to the nearest bookstore.

As I meander, I spot my father's latest book faced-out in the New and Notable display. I pick up a copy of *Man's War with the Ocean* and thumb through it. A reviewer on the back cover calls it "startling and scary." *The New York Review of Books* deems it, "a must read for anyone who cares about our planet." *Entertainment Weekly* calls him, "The Dr. Oz of the Ocean World."

In the author photo my father looks like Ryan Gosling and Bradley Cooper's love child with his shadowy stubble and Hollywood teeth. What makes me think I'm entitled to claim this man as my father?

This is all Shelly's fault. I reach into my shorts and gobble a handful of generic TUMS.

I place my father's book back on the shelf. If our face to face goes badly I don't want to own anything he wrote.

A bright blue spine among the writing books catches my eye. *Hooked: write fiction that grabs readers at page one and never lets them go*, by Les Edgerton. I flip through the chapters and notice the author has also included writing exercises. I buy it, along with a copy of *Station Eleven* that Shoe had recommended.

It's 11:39.

In the coffee shop I order coffee and grab a table near the entrance. Sitting on the booth side of the table, I begin reading from *Hooked*. Almost immediately I pull out a pen and underline things the author says about writing. Some of it Theo told us in class, and I wonder if that lying piece of shit stole all his ideas from *this* guy.

According to the author, a story starts at "the event that upsets the situation and pushes it to the breaking point…"

I've had so many breaking points my story could start anywhere, beginning with my illegitimate birth and a succession of stepfathers.

I pull out my notebook and scrawl the opening for an imaginary memoir piece I will never write.

My sister Annie's father's death unloaded a shit storm for me and my family. Bad grammar, dude. Really bad sentence.

My stepfather's murder unloaded a shit storm for my family. Do I really want to go there?

My brother's moving in with his own father made me realize our mother was beyond repair. Nope. Can't go there, either.

Getting arrested was the catalyst for me to learn who I am. Dude, cliché. I scratch this out.

Getting arrested was not the highlight of my life. Duh.

I was supposed to just help clean the school all summer, but I discovered the hows and whys of my identity. WTF?

Getting arrested should have led me down a dark path, but it led me to Shelly.

I'm tempted to scratch that out. Thinking of her is a spear in my side, but I leave it. I wouldn't be sitting here if it weren't for Shelly.

Contacting my father incites a whole slew of unknowns. Now we're getting somewhere.

I opened a can of worms that my mother tried to keep hidden in a vault for almost twenty years. No shit, Sherlock.

The mound of crap inside my mother's house grew to mountainous heights, and by scaling it, I finally excavated the key to my identity.

The mound of crap inside my mother's house grew as large as Mount Everest, but by excavating it, I finally found the key to my identity buried underneath.

Okay, I think I'm getting the hang of this.

The writing workshop got me to Seattle, but I really came here to meet the man who may or may not be my father.

In a bookstore cafe two-thousand-six-hundred miles from home, I wait... I tap the side of my head with my pen. What *am* I waiting for? The Hollywood ending?

What the hell am I doing here?

It's like that day Jeff and I got lost in the woods and some strange dude started tracking us. It was one of those summer days where the humidity clung like a sweater. We took a hike to cool off. Like idiots, we forgot to bring a canteen or food. And we were thirteen and twelve, old enough to know better. But we didn't get worried until we realized we were lost and this dude started following us.

Jeff and I sensed something off about him. It was ninety degrees out, but this guy in the woods was dressed for deer hunting in a ball cap, jeans, and a jacket. He carried a cross bow.

"Let's get out of here," Jeff whispered.

"Did he see us?"

Jeff shrugged. "I don't plan to hang around and find out."

The faster Jeff and I ran, the louder we heard footfalls echoing behind us. We thrashed our way through the trees, getting eaten by mosquitoes. Suddenly, the woods ended at a twenty-foot drop in a river.

"What do we do now?" I asked.

"We jump!"

"Are you crazy? We don't know deep it is!"

Jeff grabbed my shirt. "We either stay here and get murdered by a maniac or die trying, It's our only way out."

Trees rustled nearby. "Come on!" he said. "One. Two. Three!"

There was no turning back. My throat filled with bile, I squeezed my eyes shut, and leapt.

I'm sensing that same danger now.

According to the clock, my father will be here in less than fifteen minutes. There's no time to escape. I place my pen on the page and keep writing.

"Michael?"

I glance up. It's like looking at a fun house mirror. The man in front of me wears a weathered version of my face, a Led Zeppelin T-shirt, and cargo shorts. A pair of mirrored shades dangles from his collar. The lines on his face are roadmaps.

"I guess you know who I am." He sits in a white cafe chair across from me and I close my notebook.

"Yes," my voice creaks out. I'm not sure I'm breathing.

"Homework for your workshop?"

I nod, afraid of how my voice will sound.

"I see you've already ordered coffee," he says. "I'll get a cup and be right back. Can I bring you anything?" I shake my head.

"Dr. Meadows!" The barista says. "Are you here for another book event?"

"Not this time. I'm just having coffee with someone."

"It's good to see you again. I loved your new book."

"Thank you."

As my father places his order, I stash my papers and pen inside my backpack, quickly refill my coffee cup, and sit back down. I take a swig, hoping the hot liquid will stimulate my faulty vocal chords.

He sits across from me with a mug and a scone. After cyber-stalking him for nearly a year it's surreal to see him in the flesh. I memorized his body language and voice from his TED talk. Close up, his longish hair is streaked with gray, but I'd know him anywhere.

"Do you still run?" I ask. Really? *Those* are the first words you say to the guy you've looked for all your life?

"I do." He squints. "How did you know that?"

"I found old yearbooks."

"Ah, right." He pulls the scone apart and takes a bite. He has a long, thin scar on the back of his left hand, and his knuckles are red and craggy. He washes the scone down with his creamed coffee.

He unfolds a note from his back pocket and slides it across the table. "So, let's talk about this."

It's the message I sent him.

"You seemed to have unearthed a lot of information about me." He dips another chunk of his scone in his coffee and eats it. "My wife is a librarian, and she also tracked down a few details about you."

"I'm not after money or anything if that's what you're afraid of," I say. "I know you're famous and all..."

He finishes chewing, claps the crumbs off his hands, and wipes his mouth with a napkin. He leans in. "Then why *did* you contact me?"

"I...uh." My voice gets stuck in my throat. All my life my father has been this imaginary superhero, the guy on the white horse who would vanquish my enemies. He'd hand me a sword and a map of the world and be the one to rescue me.

But the man across the table is just a stranger eating a scone.

"I guess I just needed to see you in person." Good one, Michael. Now the Dr. Oz of the Ocean World thinks you're here to get his damn autograph. Epic. Fail.

He nods, dunks the last chunk of pastry in his cup. "Before meeting *you* in person, I needed to verify who you were, so I spent a little time in Ohio last week."

"You went to Rooster?" My heart taps out a tribal beat inside my chest.

"I did." His mouth forms a weak smile. "I hadn't been back there since, well, you know my situation. I believe you called it a 'confluence of tragedies.'" He sips his coffee. "Accurate term, by the way. You have a very precise vocabulary."

"I read a lot." I'm sweating like I ran a 10K.

"I gathered that," he says. "That's part of why I asked to meet you in a bookstore." He lifts his mug to drink. "Is this your first time in here?"

"No, I came for a reading my first night in Seattle."

He glances around. "Jen and I spend a lot of time and money in here. Jennifer's my wife."

"The librarian," I say. He nods. "Did you meet her in a bookstore?"

He sets his coffee down, rests his elbows on the table, and clasps his hands. "Actually, I met her when I did a presentation in her high school auditorium."

"Like your TED talk?"

"It was a different topic, but yes, kind of like my TED talk. I used her library's AV equipment, and afterward, when I helped her tear down, she and I started talking, and the rest, they say, is history."

We share a moment of awkward silence. I wonder if he's having as hard a time looking at me as I am at him.

"As I said, my wife did some detective work. You weren't that hard to find once she discovered your arrest and expulsion."

I wince. My arrest will live forever on YouTube.

"Jen reminded me how you teenagers are technically brain damaged, so the impulse to bring a bomb to school…"

"It was fireworks," I interject. "One of the firecrackers I had taken to school fell out of my book bag and everyone freaked out. And I wasn't trying to blow up the school. Just my ex-best-friend's car."

"Over a girl?"

I tilt my head. There is a mute understanding between us, a secret code of manhood. *Women!* "Yeah."

He settles back in his chair and grazes his fingers alongside the mug. "I have to admit I was chilled by your e-mail. It felt as if someone had infiltrated my past. How did you learn so many details? Did your mother tell you?"

I gulp some coffee. "No. In fact, she doesn't even know I found you."

"Does she know you're in Seattle?"

"She thinks I'm here for the workshop."

He tightens his lips into a horizontal line. "Who did tell you?"

"We…I found an old diary of hers that spelled out the story."

He sits forwards and tents his fingers, looks me right in the eyes. "I have nothing but fond memories of Susan. She was sweet, kind, and pretty, and I wish I'd been a better person and treated her more fairly. I never meant to hurt her, but back then we were also brain damaged teenagers."

I don't respond. He hooks his hand around the cup handle. "I sense you're angry at me."

"Did you know she was pregnant?"

My father crinkles his forehead. "She didn't tell me. In fact, I didn't see your mother again after finals week, and I'm sorry about how things turned out for her."

I look down at my coffee mug. "Well, I *was* angry at you. You should have seen the notes I *didn't* send."

He grips his cup and lifts it. "I'm ready for a refill. How about you?"

We both stand and he and I are the same height. It's remarkable to resemble someone. My brother looks like his dad and my sister has her father's coloring and Mom's features.

At the refill station, my father pumps French roast in his cup and adds cream. I choose the African blend and add cinnamon.

We sit back down.

"What happened to your family after your father...you know?" I ask.

"Drove into the lake?" He sighs. "Shortly afterward my mother was forced to liquidate any assets. Lucky for me my parents had set aside college money for all three of us. I tried to give mine back, but she refused it."

After a pause I realize the woman he's talking about is also my grandmother. The grandmother I *do* know, Grandma Barb, is just as crazy as Mom. Maybe *this* grandmother is normal. "Is your mother still alive?"

"Yes. She's happily remarried and living in Florida,"

"How about your brother and sister?"

"Nancy lives in New York, and Ed lives near D.C."

"So, once you left for college you never went back to Rooster?"

"I hadn't been to Rooster in nearly twenty years," he says. "My siblings and I have all avoided the place."

"Your old house is a restaurant now."

"I know. Jen and I ate lunch there. We drove by the old high school, too, but it was replaced with a new building near the old site. We weren't going to go in, but then I saw Earl the custodian walking around outside. He hasn't changed a bit."

I grin. "Did he recognize you?"

"He did," he says. "I was friends with his son Foster, but he and I lost track of one another. I pretty much severed ties with Rooster. Anyway, when I asked about you, Earl told me you and your sister live with him."

I slug some coffee and nod. "Did Earl figure out why you were asking about me?"

"He noted the resemblance between us." My father slings an arm across the back of his seat and clears his throat. "Earl said you lived in your car before he took you in, and that your half-sister lived on the back porch."

I lower my head so my father doesn't see my reddening face. "Did he also tell you why Annie and I couldn't live at home anymore?"

"He did." He takes a gulp of his French roast. "Is your mother getting help for her hoarding?"

"Paul...do you remember Paul Nolan?" He nods. "Paul's pretty much the only person Mom will talk to these days. He's gotten her to see a counselor who might help her clean the place. Otherwise she'll be evicted and lose everything."

"I'm sorry to hear that," he says. "Did your mother marry Paul? I remember they dated in school."

"No. He's my brother Jeff's dad, but Paul has his own family." The drummer is thumping inside my chest again. "You didn't try to see my mother while you were in Rooster, did you?"

"No. Jen and I drove by her home, but from what Earl told me, I thought it best not to disturb her."

The thumping calms after a few beats.

Okay, Michael, what more do I want to know about this guy? "What made you choose Marine Biology?"

He cracks a big smile. "Jacques Cousteau was my idol when I was a kid. There was a *National Geographic* book in the library about him, and it was filled with photos of his expeditions. He seemed like the happiest man on earth. I wanted to *be* him."

"I think that book's still there. I remember shelving it a couple times when I was a library aide."

"Is Mrs. Morgan still the librarian?"

I nod.

He takes another sip of coffee. "Are you enjoying the writing workshop? I understand it's pretty intense."

"It is. Overall, I'm glad I did it." Other than the business with Theo and Shelly.

He writes bestselling books, and I'm a writer-in-training, yet my father and I have run out of words. We both look at anything but each other.

Nearby in the Children's section a store employee is reading out loud to a group of kids. The couple next to us chatters in a foreign language. *Think, Michael. You're leaving in a few days. This may be the one and only time you see this guy. What else do you need to know?*

My father's website offers loads of information about his expeditions and books, but nothing about his personal life. I clear my throat, and ask, "Do you guys have kids?"

He folds his arms and tilts back. "You could call them that. Jen and I are owned by two very spoiled dogs and a wandering cat."

A tall, attractive woman with short brown hair approaches. She's carrying a canvas bag heavy with books. My father extends his arm and wraps it around her waist. "Jennifer Meadows, this is Michael Flynn."

Chapter Forty-Two
Michael

I stand at the podium for my final reading. The two beers I drank after dinner seem to have worn off, and I'm way more nervous than on open mic night.

It could be because this is my final chance to impress my teachers.

Or it may be that my father is in the audience.

Shoe, Dharma, Axe, and many of my friends sit in the front rows, waiting their turns to read tonight. I don't look for Theo, but I know he's there.

"Good evening," I say. "My name is Michael Gillam Flynn. The piece I'm going to read tonight is one that has taken me nineteen years to write. I'd like to thank everyone here at Hugo House Summer of Writing, particularly Frank Barnes for showing me that, while the truth is treacherous, it will also free you. And I'd also like to thank Dean Saunders for helping me understand the importance of metaphor."

I clear my throat, and begin. "This piece is called *My Father's Son.*

In a bookstore cafe two thousand six hundred and six miles from home I wait to meet the man who is my father. It's quite possible he will stand me up because he didn't seek me out. I found him.

If he's changed his mind about meeting me I bought a book to keep me company.

I don't mind being alone. As the eldest of three children I've become adept at taking care of myself. Our mother was absent either physically or emotionally, so my siblings relied on me to make sure shoes were tied and hair was combed and none of us was wearing something too dreadful.

This meeting might be a disaster. The man who may be my father and I haven't spoken on the phone, yet I know his voice from his TED talk. I know his stature and his movement. I will resemble him in twenty years. Digitized, my father seems an amiable sort, but each of us wears many faces. He might be an ogre in person.

Other than a brief note I sent him, he knows nothing about me. Being a loner, my tendency is to reserve the deepest parts of me for a deserving few. I told this man nothing about me in my letter other than my name. And that he is my father.

Almost a month passed after my initial contact, and I suspected he either thought I was a crackpot or my email went into his Spam folder.

But last night he responded.

And here I am, waiting for the man whose DNA took root inside me.

A small part of me hopes he blows this off. I can go home and live my beige life and pretend I never found him. But a large part of me hopes he shows up.

I distract myself by writing the opening of an imaginary essay about meeting my father. I write I am sitting in a bookstore cafe two thousand six hundred miles from home waiting for the man who may or not be my father. Then I hear him say my name.

I look up. All the air inside me escapes and I have forgotten how to speak. I am far from the shore, about to sink when I gulp enough air to power my voice. "Yes."

This man, my father, and I tread the waters carefully. We remain afloat, fueled by suspicion of one another's' intentions.

A river lies between us, until his wife Jennifer appears and weaves a boat to bring us safely ashore. She speaks the language of books and words, the first language of her husband's son. The three of us are rescued from the sea together, held inside a large net.

And now I have a decision to make. In two days, I'm supposed to take a red eye back to Ohio. Flying doesn't thrill me, all that thrashing and clattering at thirty thousand feet above land.

I pause, glance at the audience, and take a deep breath.

But that's not the reason I hesitate.
My father has asked me to stay.

#

Acknowledgements

While authors create the first drafts of our stories alone, we depend on the input from fellow writers and treasured readers to refine the tales. When seeking opinions, I chose people willing to be brutally honest, pointing out plot holes, typos, and bad sentences.

Katherine Grace Bond and her WIP novel group saw an early draft of this book and provided detailed comments, particularly Aaron Bond, Alex Lee, and Tammy Buskirk Deschamps. Fellow YA author Christine Rhodeback Kohler also gave me terrific feedback on an early draft.

I want to thank Valerie Stein, Laurie Zaleski, and Cat Skoor for sitting across the table from me in the (now closed) Aloha Cafe as we ignored one another and wrote. While I haven't found another perfect coffee shop, The Barnes& Noble Café at Alderwood is a close second.

The following people read excerpts or entire drafts and expressed their thoughts: Elizabeth Christy, Debbie Hardin Day, Ted Dalen, Amy Gibson, Angela Hendershot, Ted Gavarkavich, Erica George, Margo Kelly, Steven Parlato, Cynthia Rucker, Leslie Skoda, Cindy Sterling, Karen McKay Wardle, Beverly Watson. I'd also like to thank David and Donnas Moe (even though they shared a typo-ridden bad draft with their neighbors without my permission!!!)

I'd like to thank fans of BREAKFAST WITH NERUDA, who demanded to know what happens next, and also my characters Michael and Shelly, who appeared in my dreams and insisted their story was not finished.

Finally, I owe a huge debt to my awesome critique partners: Jennifer Bardsley, Louise Cypress, Penelope Wright, and Sharman Badgett-Young. This book is all your fault!

Pablo, as always, you're my treasured writing partner.

AUTHOR'S NOTE

While many locations and events cited in this novel are real, Rooster, Ohio, The Hugo House Summer of Writing Workshop, and Emerald City Books are fictional.

If you enjoyed **BLUE VALENTINES**, Michael and Shelly's story continues in **THE LANGUAGE OF THE SON**

Here's a sneak preview.

Chapter One

July

My father crouches nose to nose with Jack, his seven-year-old Golden Lab, as they mock wrestle in the back yard. I'm a little jealous because he's never played with me like that, but I have no right to be; he's known the dog longer.

Two weeks ago, when I moved in with my father, I imagined conversations where we talked about books and movies and compared memories of Rooster, Ohio. So far, none of the films inside my head have followed the script.

His wife Jennifer stands next to me at the French doors. "Your father morphs into a big kid when it comes to Jack. Lucy, Jennifer's black and white Boston terrier, trots over and she picks the dog up and they nose kiss. "I'd be willing to bet if he had to choose between me and Jack, the dog would probably win."

She sets Lucy down. "I'm headed out to get a haircut. Do you want to go with me? There's a Barnes & Noble near the salon."

I glance at my father and imagine more of our awkward dialogue—or more precisely—our silences.

Conversations with him are like throwing darts in the dark.

"Yeah, I'll come."

Jennifer steps outside and Lucy shimmies next to her to the back yard. "Ash, I'm going out, and taking Michael with me."

My father looks up, blows her a kiss, and yanks at a rubber rhinoceros inside his dog's jaw. He doesn't even glance at me.

Jennifer hands me her keys. "I'll let you drive if you like."

I give her a big smile. "Awesome. I like taking the bus, but I also miss driving. In Rooster, if you want to go anywhere you *have* to drive."

"There aren't any buses there?"

"They only run in the center of town, and not very often."

"Do people bike?" she asks.

"Not if they want to live long."

She laughs, and we head out to the garage. Her shiny, red Toyota Camry isn't even the same species as The Blue Whale.

As Jennifer gets her hair cut, I browse the magazine section of the bookstore and do a double take at the cover of *People* magazine. Ryan Gosling has the same highbrow, shadowy stubble, and chiclet teeth as my father. *I* look like my father. So why the hell don't women fawn over *me* like they do Gosling? or my father? Oh yeah, because I'm kind of a nerd.

I start perusing the bookstore shelves.

In the poetry section *100 Love Sonnets* by Pablo Neruda reminds me of Shelly. Don't want to think about her. That ship has sailed and hit an iceberg.

I head to nonfiction where several of my father's books occupy half a shelf. He's everywhere. On paper anyway.

After an hour of browsing, I choose a writing guide called *Ron Carlson Writes a Story* and a gift to send to my sister Annie: *100 Great Novels to Read Before You Die*.

Jennifer walks in as I'm in line to pay. "Do you mind if I look around a little?" she asks.

"Not at all." I'm never in a hurry to leave a bookstore, even a half-assed one like Barnes and Noble. "I'll wait in the cafe."

As a school librarian, you'd think Jennifer would be sick of books, but most of their bookcases at home are full. And she'll read pretty much anything. The other day I caught her reading *Fifty Shades of Grey* in the backyard.

"This book is hysterical," she said, when I handed her a bottle of water from the fridge. "It's so bad I can't put it down."

"Are you learning anything?"

She closed the book and unscrewed the cap on her water. "Don't worry. I won't tie your father up and whip him." She winked. "At least when you're in the house."

While Jennifer shops, I pour myself a free cup of water and find a seat. The book I bought for Annie lists a couple of my favorites, *The Grapes of Wrath* and *Heart of Darkness,* but I don't see *Shadow of the Wind. On the*

Road made the cut. Shelly's favorite book. The one that binds her to Theo.

That two-timing-lying-asshole and my latest nemesis.

It seems the people I care about most betray me. Rick. Shelly. Theo. I wonder who's next.

As much as she hurt me, not being with Shelly every day is like phantom pain, as if I'm missing a leg yet I still want to run.

I was also supposed to be back in Ohio two weeks ago, but after I met my father for the first time, he and Jennifer asked me to stay.

I thought remaining in Seattle was the answer to everything. I wouldn't have to encounter Shelly and I'd get to know my father.

Now I'm not so sure.

END SAMPLE

About the Author

Author, radio host, and writing teacher **Laura Moe** spent most of her working life as a librarian and English teacher in central and Southeastern Ohio, but moved to Seattle where she writes full-time and is an active member of SCBWI and EPIC Group Writers. Moe is the author of BREAKFAST WITH NERUDA (Simon & Schuster/Merit Press, 2016) named by the New York Public Library as one the Best Books for Teens in 2016. She is owned by a spoiled white cat named Pablo.

For book discussion questions, Michael's college essay, and other examples of writing from his writing workshop, visit Laura's website: www.lauramoebooks.com

Twitter @Lauramoewrter

instagram @lauramoewriter

Facebook Laura Moe writer

Made in the USA
Columbia, SC
01 July 2019